# LOVE IS THE LAW

## NICK MAMATAS

DARK HORSE BOOKS
Milwaukie

Cover design by Amy Arendts
Book design by Krystal Hennes
Published by Dark Horse Books
A division of Dark Horse Comics, Inc.
10956 SE Main Street
Milwaukie, OR 97222
DarkHorse.com
International Licensing: (503) 905-2377

Library of Congress Cataloging-in-Publication Data

Mamatas, Nick.
Love is the law / Nick Mamatas.
    pages cm
ISBN 978-1-61655-222-0
1. Single women--Fiction. 2. Murder--Investigation--Fiction. I. Title.
PS3613.A525L68 2013
813'.6--dc23

                            2013016919


First edition: September 2013
10 9 8 7 6 5 4 3 2 1
Printed in the United States of America.

*For Olivia Flint, one more time.*

# LOVE IS THE LAW

# 1.

I am a fucking genius. The only one on Long Island, guaranteed. Yes, there are scientists at Brookhaven, and at Stony Brook, charming quarks. Clever, and mathematically minded, but not geniuses. All sorts of millionaires roar across the island on the Cannonball for Friday happy hour in Amagansett in the summertime, but they were slaves to an abstraction smaller than themselves, and thus disqualified. There probably might have been a lone kook or two living in some moldy clapboard house on the shore who might almost qualify as genius. I knew I was the only genius because I was still fucking alive. Bernstein, who was a scientist, and a millionaire, and more recently a lone kook, wasn't. He was stretched across the seventies shag rug, bright orange except where his blood had pooled, in his living room. I made a note of it. The lights were on, and so was the little black-and-white television he kept balanced atop a milk crate, tuned to TV-55. Bernstein didn't have cable. On the screen, it was the usual news—East Germans gathered up by *der Antifaschistischer Schutzwall*, chanting, *"Wir bleiben hier."* The gun was near Bernstein's right hand, and chunks of his skull, and hair, and brains, did splay off to the left. Whoever killed him probably thought that the cops would be too stupid, and too relieved, to examine the scene closely. But Bernstein was left handed, and anyone who took the time to open his journals and read his many writings on Marxism and the occult, a few of which he once shared with me, would have spotted that right away. On the other hand, on the *sinister* hand,

if you get me, nobody ever lost money betting against the cops.
Local fruitcake who writes letters to the community newspaper
demanding that the North Shore proletariat rise up to defend
the gains of October sees the Eastern bloc crumble on TV,
takes off his pants, and shoots himself in the head. Case closed:
happens all the time.

Bernstein lived in a little two-room shed right on the
southern part of Mount Sinai Harbor. He could have sold it
and been rich, but he didn't care about such things. He liked
the swamp, the hills, the fingery tree branches in the late
autumn. Bernstein had once read a poem, an original compo-
sition, to that effect at the Good Read Book Stop. That was
in May, when I decided to put him on my route. It was an
extremely mediocre poem, but I liked Bernstein anyway.

I thought about jimmying the lock and helping myself to
some of Bernstein's rarer books and papers—he had a photo-
copy of the original handwritten *Liber AL vel Legis* he'd gotten
from a friend in Berkeley—but for a moment my Will left me
and I ran, scared, back home, the muck of the swampy backyard slurping against my Docs as if to keep me there.

What is there to say about Bernstein? He was brilliant. A
polyglot, an economist, a talented magician, a prolific corre-
spondent. Instead of a refrigerator and oven, he had three
huge file cabinets in his kitchen, filled with carbons of the
letters he sent to statesmen, wizards, revolutionaries, and
artists. And he was perceptive enough to sense me watching
him. Nobody had ever caught me before, but he immediately
knew I was outside watching him. The second night I visited
him, he marched over to the window. I ducked. He drew the
shade and then turned on a bright light. On the grass before
me I read the words NO KEY NEEDED. I turned around and saw
the letters, backwards and made of black tape, on the shade.
I made to run, but he slammed his fist against the wall and

opened the shade. So I walked around to the front and entered
the unlocked door. My look was so distinctive that running
was useless anyway.

"What are you called?" he asked me.

"Aimee," I said. It was the first name that came to mind.

He scowled and said, "Amaranth it is."

"Huh?"

"Bloom, O ye Amaranths! bloom for whom ye may," he
said. "For me ye bloom not! Glide, rich streams, away!" He
raised a finger and said, "Coleridge!" Then he told me to sit
down. My boots had steel toes. I had a ring with a spike on
it in my pocket, and put my hand in my pocket just in case,
but I sat down.

Bernstein had a film projector—that was the light he had
used—and whipped the sheet from his couch and showed me
a Super 8 print of an old weird black-and-white film called
*Meshes of the Afternoon*. It was strange and short, like an
MTV video, except silent and about . . . I still don't know. It
was like a dream, I guess. Not like a dream sequence in an
ordinary Hollywood movie, but like an actual dream. Maya
Deren, the director and "star," was a commie gone occultist
too. She was beautiful, with a haystack of black curls. Why
wouldn't the *lwa* want to ride her, kiss her till her lips were
chapped and bleeding? Bernstein had a nice cock and paid
me to suck it. I was not a whore, though. I just needed the
money, and was patient with him, not like a whore would be.
It always took him hours to get off. He hummed to himself,
patted the bald side of my head, murmured the magic words,
then let his *ov* into my mouth. Bernstein would have given
me anything I wanted for nothing in return, but then I would
have really been his whore, his slave, dependent on him the
way a sheep is on its shepherd. He was a good yogi, but
couldn't stretch far enough to suck his own dick. So it was

commerce without capital for him, magick without tears for me. He never tried to touch me, or make me get naked. We weren't boyfriend and girlfriend, or mentor and protégé. Maybe I was his Scarlet Woman; perhaps he was my Holy Guardian Angel, but in the final analysis, we were comrades, a cadre in an Imaginary Party.

I lived with my grandmother and given my haircut and sartorial choices—punk as fuck, studs and ripped everything, a bright orange Mohawk and I didn't give a fuck about my "figure" either—I wasn't going to get a job at the Smith Haven Mall, or even Farpoint Comics. My mother was dead, my father's new wife was a crack pipe and he was better at sucking that than I was at sucking cock. When Maya walked into a room to see herself sleeping on a recliner, I felt something important. When I saw her fling herself against first one wall, then another, as she tried to climb up a flight of crooked, swaying steps, I knew what it was. For so long my other world, my alternative existence, was in Manhattan. Whenever I could, I'd get out to the city on the LIRR. Two hours on the train and then a quick stride into the Village, to Bleecker Bob's Records, St. Mark's Bookshop, a vegetarian bakery, shawarma, the dirty and foul Mars Bar where I learned to drink. But all I was doing was buying, then leaving. I was the worst sort of commodity fetishist; in trying to consume the life I wanted, all I was eating was my own slow death. With Bernstein, I realized that I could make my life my own, on Long Island or anywhere else. *Wir bleiben hier.* We are staying here.

But someone killed my Bernstein, and ruined absolutely everything. But I am a fucking genius, and I was determined to find out who killed Bernstein and bring them to . . .

No, not to justice. To something else.

# 2.

I have mastered only one feat of magick, specifically the art of invisibility. Bernstein saw right through it, of course, but otherwise it worked pretty well. It's easy enough to be invisible on Long Island—be a pedestrian. Sidewalks here are few and far between, so every walk is a nature walk. Usually dead nature. A dead bird is an awful thing to stumble across, as they always seem to die with their eyes open and staring. At me. It's startling to see one at your feet, and even worse to hear the crunch of thin bones underfoot, but the worst is the walk back. The shock of the unexpected decays into a dread of seeing the body again. *Is this where that thing was? No, it must have been further along the road.* Then the ground gives way by just an inch. I look down at my shoes. No, I was right.

Roadkill on the street proper or in the sandy strip on the shoulders of most roads is nearly as bad. Dead mammals make a larger splash—imagine wrapping a paint can full of sausage casings in a mink stole, and smashing it to the ground. I remember one dead raccoon whose glassy-eyed stare seemed almost wise. It was finals week, and I had been run ragged, having signed up for nineteen credits. I walked by the carcass every day, wishing I could feel as serene as it looked, even with its viscera splayed around the body like torn wrapping paper. Serenity is the key to this ritual.

At first, there wasn't a single day when I wasn't harassed or accosted by drivers and passengers in passing cars. Some just scream. Others shout, "Ha, you're poor!" or "Get a car!"

or "Fucking freak!" or, after the song became popular, "Punk rock girl!" I got quite a few comments about my sexual preferences, with a level of detail that wouldn't be more exacting had I been pushing a naked lover in front of me in a wheelbarrow. One guy even shouted, "Hey, nipple clips!" at me. After a heavy rain, or during a light one, some drivers liked to veer toward the side of the road and kick up a wall of gutter water.

The answer was to walk more, and to walk calmly. No more shouting back, no more shaking my fist or even grabbing a stone and flinging it at the rear windshield, then running off across the railroad tracks or into a yard when the brake lights flared angry red and the car stopped. I'd just take it, and prowl the nights. I walked a mile and a half to school, tromping through snowdrifts or marching under the blazing sun with nothing but an outstretched arm and a palm toward heaven to shade me. I was everywhere, all the time. Did people see me on the shoulder of the highway today or yesterday? Had I been striding across their lawn last week or last summer, walking on the Port Jeff pier with an ice cream cone on the Fourth of July or Memorial Day? Had I been spotted heading off the train at Huntington and taking the long stroll to the Angle, or Cinema Arts Centre when they were on the way to the movies, or when they'd been coming back from the movies? I dyed my hair the Little Orphan Annie orange and got a boy's leather jacket, just to be more distinctive. Even the hardcore bands on LI—all boys, of course—dressed in backwards baseball caps and Gap jeans, so I was That Ugly Fucking Girl. Because I was everywhere, I eventually was nowhere. Part of the scenery, just another tree or strip mall.

And I sang to myself. Subvocalizations that set my sinuses ringing. I loved Token Entry and SFA and Ludichrist, who actually knew how to play their instruments. They were local, and the tapes were cheap, and I played them till they snapped or demagnetized. I knew better than to wear headphones in traffic, so I was my own grumbling, scatting Walkman. The music kept my heart rate accelerated, but even. I felt like I could do anything, and I started doing just that. I liked to keep a hand on my little spiked ring, though it wasn't even all that good for stabbing people. But it helped me feel prepared, ready for anything. Never listened to anything mainstream except for that one Public Enemy song that everyone loved that summer. *Nineteen eighty-niiiiiiiiine!*

Once I achieved invisibility, it was easy to indulge in my hobby. I liked to walk up to the big bay windows that so many of the more obnoxious houses around here had and peer in. I had my favorites. The Dominican family living on Route 25A was one. The father's name was Raymundo. *Ray* plus *mundo*—I daydreamed that his name meant "light of the world" because I found portent and sign in everything I observed. Raymundo loved to chase his kids around, yelping and laughing and pretending to be a werewolf. His wife was a dried-up little woman who shrieked and complained and didn't speak any English. The kids, three boys and a girl, were all chubby and snotty. Raymundo worked at Fairchild building Warthogs and other imperialist death weapons, until there wasn't a Fairchild anymore, and then he wasn't happy anymore. Bernstein would have somehow blamed Gorbachev for such a thing, were he around to do so. Raymundo stayed home and fumed at his big television set, and got fat and stupid; then one day they were all gone and the walls were bare except for the square stains where the kids' school pictures had been.

I had a few people up in Belle Terre, a tiny village of mansions built around a country club. They weren't as exciting as I'd hoped. No long cocktail parties or feather boas or insane ranting over a ticker tape à la Gomez Addams. One couple about the age of my parents ate the same shitty Pathmark frozen pizza that I did, except that they had a huge kitchen with a great slate island on which to put their paper plates and greasy napkins. No kids; presumably they couldn't birth any that would match their furniture, so decided against. According to their mail, the family name was Riley. The wife never seemed to receive any correspondence, but the dude was Robert. Robert Riley—he could have been a comic book superhero with that name.

And then there was one old woman in Belle Terre who did nothing all night but watch the BBC feed sucked down from space via an enormous satellite dish behind her cabana and weep into a handkerchief. She kept strange hours to keep up with the television, taking tea at 11 p.m. She slept on the couch in the afternoons. A black maid cleaned around her twice a week, clearing the piles of saucers and other service items.

High school dirtbags were endlessly fascinating as well. Port Jefferson is a mix of suburban developments and older cottages and saltboxes. Dirtbags and longhairs lived with a parent or two in the latter. Only the most pathetic and poor, like me and my grandmother, lived in actual apartments. Dirtbags loved their stereos, and really could stare at an Iron Maiden album cover for an hour as the album played, as the aluminum siding against which I huddled as I peered through the window buzzed along with the rhythm section. Sometimes, a few of them got together and played a half-hearted game of Dungeons & Dragons. They loved the occult shit, these kids, but not one of them had the discipline necessary for real magick. In school, we never spoke. There was a bright red line between punk and metal, just as there was between dirtbag and Guido, Guido and preppy. Every year we marched out to the football field and took a class picture, all bunched together in our groups, with the few Asian or Hispanic kids around even further out on the periphery. I took a lipstick to the picture and drew the borders between us all, tracing out a perfect unicursal hexagram, as though right from the pen of Aleister Crowley. Picture a diamond with a bow tie, or something like two of the little spaceships from *Asteroids* laid atop one another—one pointing toward the Divine, the other toward the Abyss. Just like high school. I was glad to be invisible, happy that the relationships with my classmates were utterly imaginary. I'd even ditched school the day of the picture, and wasn't in it.

I used my power to get my hands on occult books. The public library only had the usual Wiccan shit from Raymond Buckland and born-again Christian scare books that were totally hysterical in both senses of the word. And there was Good Read Book Stop, but more about that later. SUNY Stony Brook's college library—just fifteen minutes away— had a few good volumes, and I was able to walk right in to the stacks despite not having a student ID card. I'd just wait for a student who looked like she might have been a friend, and walk in behind them. A lot of the books had already been stolen—anything by Crowley goes quick, as does anything that has pentagrams and other magical circles printed on the pages, or anything that looked old. But I found a few good ones, and took them. Crowley's *777: vel prolegomena symbolica ad systemam sceptico-mysticae viae explicandae, fundamentum hieroglyphicum sanctis- simorum scientiae summae* is a favorite. It took me a week to memorize the title, and I didn't even allow myself to open the book until I did. And on the first page I read, "Am I no better than a staphylococcus because my ideas still crowd in chains? But we digress." And I howled with glee, my first real laugh since moving in with Grandma. As far as the rest of it, I had no idea what the fuck he was on about. *777* is sort of a farmer's almanac without any explanations. I saw Chinese trigrams, and a chart that tied human hips and thighs to centaurs—I presumed because that's where man meets horse in a centaur body, but it was just confusing. It was a great edition though, published in London in a limited edition of five hundred copies in 1909, the year my grandmother was born in Brooklyn. When it came to comprehension though, I was no better than a staphylococcus.

Bernstein was such a *godsend*—and even now I struggle not to think in terms like godsend. I'd gone to the bookstore not to hear Valium-addled housewives read their poems, but to find some beginner Crowley titles and boost them. Instead I found Bernstein. His poems were just as bad as anyone else's, but he knew it. He was a prankster, mocking the other readers. I didn't dare laugh and give it all away. Though he was a wiry little man with gray hair shooting out from the top of his head like a dandelion, I sat there with my legs together and got wet for him. He knew me inside out. He let me be "Aimee" for a week or two before he casually admitted that he knew my name was Dawn. That I'd graduated from high school and had no particular plans. That he knew my father once, when they were younger.

So, who killed Bernstein? Who could? Of course he had enemies. Intelligent people always have enemies. He certainly didn't have any friends, save me and his far-flung correspondents. He was up to his eyebrows in politics too. That summer, a lot of his time had been spent on the phone to Yugoslavia, shouting in three languages, and to Western Union, sending money over to middlemen in France. My eyes would roll to the back of my head during one of his spontaneous lectures on the number of dishwashing

machines in Moscow, and how the bureaucratic caste domi-
nating the deformed workers' states were ready to be
destroyed by the *real* proletarian revolution. Maybe it was
a good thing he's dead.

I couldn't call the police. I couldn't bear the thought of the
fucking pigs going through Bernstein's papers and library.
And I'd have to explain what I'd been doing outside, peering
in through the window—one of our many little games. Plus,
the cops are generally under the thumb of either the bosses
or some occult group. I could pick up the phone, dial 911,
and report the crime to the murderer, or one of his mind
slaves. And then there's the gibberish ideology of the bourgeois legal system in the first place. How would a Christian
choose to punish the Roman soldier with the hammer and
three nails, if he could?

There's a ritual I know—*Liber III vel Jugorum*. It's
freedom through bondage. Set a rule: don't use a word like
*the*, or *but*. Or don't use the letter *m*. And when you do, take
a razor to your flesh. Soon enough you'll stop doing what
you've decided not to do. So what I barred myself from even
thinking was the word, the concept of *justice*. Nothing's
fair. Nobody is owed jack shit. Every dumb failure, from
premenstrual cramps to hearing only the outro of that one
song on WLIR that I so wanted to tape, is exactly what I
had coming. And the same with television. Hurricane Hugo
tore through North Carolina and every weepy redneck hick
appealed to God, and it was hilarious. I did slip up a few
times. Every chubby girl on Long Island cuts herself when
she's feeling angsty—vomiting is for mere cheerleaders—
but I worked with a deeper purpose, running a razor across
my stomach, playing with fingertips full of blood. It hurt
all the time, but that's the point. After a week, I was free of
notions of bourgeois j_____. I couldn't even imagine

anything but a dark and swirling hole, a mouth of a great wyrm yawning wide to consume us all, whenever I even tried to think of that unthinkable thing. A second feat of magick, accomplished.

# 3.

A tree fell through Bernstein's house when the remnant of Hugo hit Long Island. I had imagined having a few days or even a week of surreptitiously collecting the mail in the hope of finding a clue before the neighbors figured out something was up and called the pigs. Instead, the front page of *Newsday* told the story to everyone on Long Island. Jerome Bernstein, "former" sixties radical and "New Age" believer—two errors in just three words!—was found dead when a LILCO linesman checking out nearby power lines noticed the small cottage under a large tree and decided to investigate. Bernstein had committed suicide via self-inflicted gunshot wound, and "a note may have been found." The tree and the wind must have cast some of Bernstein's letters onto the lawn and all throughout the nearby wood.

I made toast and eggs for my grandmother and read the paper at our tiny Formica table. Everything smelled like grease and smoke, and made me sick to my stomach. Once upon a time I was a vegetarian, which drove Grandma crazy. Bernstein used to smirk at me and call me a "Pop-Tarts and french fry vegetarian," which was true enough. Then I gave it up.

"I know that man," Grandma said. She rarely spoke anymore. I lived with her for one reason—her Social Security checks kept the lights on, and Section 8 paid the rent. She lived with me for lots of reasons, even though half the time she looked at me like I was some kind of monster born of senile dementia—I did the laundry, cooked a little, let her watch TV till her hair fell out from the radiation. She pointed to the front page of the newspaper. "Christmas Jerome."

"Christmas Jerome . . . ? His last name was Bernstein," I said.

"Billy brought him to the house one Christmas," Grandma said. "Because the poor boy had nowhere else to go. They were in college together, at Stony Brook." She'd been taking to calling my father, William, "Billy" again for the past few months. "He was a nice young fellow. He brought us a present he made. A strange painting of a tower. I couldn't display it, of course, but you know what they say: it's the thought that counts." She looked back down at her eggs, cooked over hard the only way I could be bothered to do them, and sliced into one with the edge of her fork. Then she glanced back up at the paper. "I know that man," she said. "Christmas Jerome . . ." I let her cycle through the story one more time, but folded the paper so she wouldn't see the picture again and perseverate even more. The story was virtually the same the second time, except that she said, "It's around here somewhere." Not likely true—half the time Grandma thought she was still living in the split-level ranch she had before the bank foreclosed on it. "Billy" had smoked his way through four months of mortgage payments. Once I found her peering into the hall closet, looking for the second story of a home she no longer had.

Dad was easy to find. There's a lot of money in Suffolk, and on the North Shore especially. There are pockets of poverty, but only one real crack house in Port Jeff. I took the car, which I always hated. Driving was just so visible; I always imagined windshields as huge magnifying glasses that inflated my head to Macy's Thanksgiving Day Parade balloon proportions. The car is supposed to be a symbol of American freedom, but it's just another way for the cops to track you. You're caged already. But Long Island barely has any public transportation thanks to that old cryptofascist Robert Moses, and the crack house was down a back road, so I had no real choice. It wasn't far from the old manor houses that lined the hill over the harbor, houses with back-yards large enough to stable a horse. After that, a few smaller homes in disrepair, their inhabitants long since driven out by high property taxes, then the crack house squat.

Nothing stirred when I pulled up in Grandma's old Volkswagen Rabbit, though the diesel engine made it sound like there were hundreds of marbles rolling around under the hood. Branches and wet leaves littered the lawn and porch. The door was locked, but it was easy enough to open with my driver's license. Dad was on a couch that had been salvaged from . . . somewhere. Dredged out of the Long Island Sound, it looked like, and smelled like. There was no TV, no lamps, and the room was dark thanks to some towels tacked up over the windows. Someone else was in the corner, stretched out on a stained twin mattress. Dad had his feet up on a coffee table made of plywood and a few milk crates, just the way he did back when he lived at home.

"Hey, Dad," I said. It took a long moment for his head to turn my way. "What's the matter—did you switch over to smack from crack?"

"Dawn . . ." he said. "What the fuck do you want?" He looked me over and sneered at me. "You're tracking mud into the house. Into my home!" Dad tried to shout like he used to, but he was desiccated in his little wifebeater T-shirt and khaki shorts, so his words just came out as a grating groan. He mumbled, "I don't have any fuckin' money for you, okay."

"I have some for you," I said. I did. Ten dollars.

Dad perked up a bit. "What do you want?" The woman on the mattress stirred as well. She smiled at me—her front teeth were missing—and stood up and lurched toward the little kitchen beyond the room in which I stood. There was an upstairs too, and I strained my ears in case more crackheads were up there. I wasn't worried. All I had to do was take a giant step backward, get into my car, and go. If that was my Will, it would be done.

"Remember your friend from high school, or something? Jerome Bernstein?"

"What about him? You want to suck his dick or something?" The girl was back from the kitchen with two plastic cups of water. She made to offer me one, from across the room, but was giggling too much at Dad's little joke to make her way over to me.

"Oh, I have sucked his dick. And it was fucking good, Daddy," I said. "I like Jew cock. Nice and clean, no dick cheese." The crackhead girl really lost it then. She spilled both cups and fell to her knees, her shoulders bobbing, her hand over her mouth as she snorted.

"So, he's dead."

"AIDS? He die of AIDS?" Dad asked. "Did that fucking kike faggot give my daughter fucking AIDS?" He slumped back onto the couch.

"Someone shot him in the head. Any idea who it might be?" I pulled the ten-dollar bill from my pocket, crumpled it up, and threw it at him. He snapped to for a moment, snatched it off his lap, and squeezed it tightly in his palm.

"Shot him, eh?" he said. To the girl, he said, "Someone shot my second-best buddy Jerome from high school. Can you imagine that? Shot him right in the fucking head."

"Second best?" For all I wanted to just strangle him right now, this was the deepest and most intimate conversation I'd had with my father in years. So fuck him. "You talk like a girl," I told him.

"There's a hierarchy in all things," Dad said, the druggie quiver leaving his voice for a moment. Then it was back. "That's why Communism ain't ever gonna work, bitch." It was his last dinner at the apartment all over again.

"So there was a painting of a tower—know anything about that?"

Dad looked at me, his eyes bright and cracked red. "That fucking thing. God, that fucking painting. It went with the house. Yeah, go look in the house." The house that the bank took, the contents that Dad couldn't sell to the thrift store having been dragged out to the curb and left. Then he murmured something more about his best friend.

"When did you last see Bernstein anyway?"

"A long time ago, hon. Long ago. Like two weeks ago."

"Where?" I couldn't imagine Bernstein having much patience for my father's bullshit. "Here?"

"Naw, naw," he said. Then he pointed to his forehead and tapped his temple twice. "I saw him up in here. In heeere." The girl cackled. Dad focused on me again. "Why ain't you in school? Is it fuckin' Halloween? I don't have any candy for you."

"I graduated last summer, Dad."

He snorted. "Why ain't you in college then, eh? You're so fucking smart with your SATs and shit. College girl. You can suck a lot of Jew dick in college." He put his hands together and rolled the ten bucks into an even tighter ball. "College fucking bitch. I went to college too, you know. And look at me now!" He laughed and laughed and spread his arms wide. "Soon, all this too will be yours."

I took a giant step backward out of the house, and got into my car and drove. At a red light, I opened the glove compartment, took out a razor, found a tear in my stocking, and left a cut on a patch of new flesh.

# 4.

The few friends I had in high school—punks like me, and the one kid who loved Lovecraft and didn't try to hit on me—were all off to their little petit-bourgeois college experiences in Massachusetts or California. That's how the system parcels out culture, and cultural capital, to reproduce the class system. And my only two living relatives were both out of their minds. But both Grandma and Dad had said some interesting things, and if Bernstein had taught me anything it is that there are no coincidences. The tower painting, and Grandma's inexplicable recall of it, meant something. Dad's dream about Bernstein, whether he actually had one or was just trying to fuck with me somehow, meant something too. I went home and checked my copy of *777*. There was a chart detailing the proper titles and looks of tarot trumps. Of course, the Tower is bad news. War unto ruin, truths revealed as lies. The revelation that blinds. But the title Crowley suggested—*The Lord of the Hosts of the Mighty*—well, that was interesting. The capitalist class; it could mean nothing else.

Capitalism is an occult formulation. Look at the back of a dollar bill, and it's all there. That's what makes the exoteric esoteric; put that shit right on display and that's how a symbol gains power. The Federal Reserve makes money out of nothing but Will every day—it's a friggin' wizards' guild. Where the pyramid meets the eye is where Bernstein was in life, and where I was now that he was dead. I'd be next with a bullet in the brain, with a gun placed in the wrong hand as a knowing joke.

When the bleeding stopped, I went on my rounds. Afternoons often meant a lot of empty houses, but nothing is more real than someone home alone, away from work or school. The best homes were the predevelopment ones, where the unemployed and underemployed stayed all day, often without air conditioning. They left the blinds up and the windows open. First, I checked in on a grotesquely ugly-cum-beautiful grad student. He was a favorite of mine. A huge Indian fellow, wild sideburns, dressed in suit jackets he couldn't button around his pendulous belly, constantly chewing on his fingernails. He was grading papers at his kitchen table. A slim Asian girl, Korean American was my guess, brought in some tea. He kissed her hand by way of thanks. I decided to come back some night to see how they fucked. I imagined she'd have to bend over the side of the bed or something. At least he'd kneel before her and put her legs up on her shoulders or something. Maybe they didn't have a sexual relationship, but just read one another poetry or something. I liked this guy a lot—when I first found him I'd made the racist error of deciding that he was in the sciences, but he was actually part of the English Department over at Stony Brook. Studying the Brontës, even. He took the bus to campus most days, filling two seats in its last row. He even smiled as he graded the papers. Probably because he wouldn't be living in Port Jefferson forever.

Next was an older woman. My grandmother didn't know her, so she must have come out here from the city fairly recently. Her lawn was unkempt, so no children to push the mower for her, and no money to hire a landscaper. She had a bay window in the front of her clapboard house and some overgrown hedges hugging the exterior wall, so I was able to squeeze in and get very close. Then my favorite thing happened. This one didn't like looking out the window. She had the couch right under the window and her television against the opposite wall. And on the show she was watching, one of the characters sat down on his couch, the camera over his shoulder, and turned on his own television. And the show the character was watching was *also* about someone watching television. I had to stifle a barbaric yawp of glee. The old lady was half-deaf—the TV was blaring, and the TV on the TV was also friggin' loud—so she didn't hear my snorting. It couldn't get any better than that, so I had to move on.

The school bus rolled down Route 25A and let some kids out. Mostly high school freshmen and sophomores, of course, as around here virtually every kid gets a car for his or her sixteenth birthday, but there was one dirtbag senior stuck taking the bus. Did Daddy take the T-bird away, or was he really a sad welfare case of some sort? I knew the kid—his name was Greg, and he had been a year behind me in school. Skinny, blond, acne scars on his cheeks visible from across the street, denim everywhere, Megadeth T-shirt rather than Metallica—clearly an intellectual among metalheads. Well over six foot as well. I had never followed him before, so it was time.

His house was too cute, and neatly kept. Two stories, but there was a tin shed in the backyard to climb on, so I'd be able to get a look even if Greg's room was upstairs. As a dirtbag, him heading right to his bedroom to put on headphones to either listen to music or practice his guitar playing was a demographic inevitability. The backyard also had a bunch of kiddie toys—a bright plastic Big Wheel, a wading pool, a dangerous-looking swing set piebald with rust stains—so perhaps I'd luck out. Families who shit out a lot of children like to keep the little kids upstairs, and will give the older child a first-floor or basement room. I hovered on the corner for a long moment, then made my move.

Greg had a basement all to himself. A little television, a pretty gigantic stereo, and vinyl and tape everywhere. His CDs were neatly filed on a bookshelf. And he was a bassist, or an aspirant anyway. Permissive parents, or he just didn't give a shit, as he ran through a lengthy tuning process on a basic Peavey practice amp. I slid down to a squat, then sat on my ass and watched Greg sidelong, so my body wouldn't drape a shadow over his room and give me away. Sweet Satan, he was practicing standing up, in front of a dusty full-length mirror. There would be no homecoming dance for this boy next week. Or maybe there would. Right atop the mirror, on a high shelf, was a small oil painting in reds and yellows—a great eye, a tower melting under the blazing flames of wisdom, dragon ascendant, shadowy figures hurtling themselves from the walls, like a figure in a faster, hellish *Nu descendant un escalier n° 2*. The Tower painting.

I slipped my spike ring on and rapped on the basement window till Greg heard me and looked up.

# 5.

Greg had cigarettes, but didn't dare smoke them in his bedroom, so we went down by the train crossing to smoke them. Cloves, which he kept hidden from his school friends because cloves are obviously for faggots. He was happy to tell me that he bought the painting at the thrift store run by the local Greek Orthodox church—"for a dollar, because they just wanted it out of there"—but was much more reticent when discussing the *why* of it all.

"Crowley Tarot," Greg said between puffs. "Wow."

"Yeah, wow," I said. "So, you didn't know? What were you even doing poking around a Christian thrift store anyway?"

Greg shrugged. "I just went."

"Ever go before?"

"No."

"Since?"

"No . . ." He looked at me. The first time he'd made extended eye contact. It was like a flagpole had turned to stare at me. Probably wasn't used to talking to girls. I made a note not to touch him in any way, as he might misinterpret it as some kind of sex signal. "Why, do you think it's cursed?"

I laughed and laughed. "No, no, it's not cursed. And even if it was cursed, here's how to neutralize the effects of the curse—stop believing in the curse."

"You don't believe in curses? Aren't you a Wiccan or something?"

"Of course not," I told him. "I'm a Marxist. A Communist."

"Well, why do you care so much about the fucking painting, if there's nothing special about it?"

So I told him almost everything. About "Christmas Jerome," the gun in the wrong hand, my father the crack-head, what I was hoping to do. I kept the details of *Liber III vel Jugorum* to myself. Greg agreed that it was some heavy shit. But there was something Greg wasn't telling me. He looked away again; he lacked the childlike excitement a moron like him should be experiencing when the talk of an afternoon turns to dead bodies and magickal secrets. He hadn't even asked what I was doing crouched outside his window.

"Want to go to Mount Sinai and see if any of Bernstein's papers got blown into the woods?" Boy howdy, did Greg want to do that. But he wasn't interested in walking, though he had no car of his own. I walked off without him. He followed eventually, hair flopping against his shoulders, face flushed.

"Tada!" Greg said as we crossed the yellow lines on Crystal Brook Hollow Road, and passed into Mount Sinai. I swallowed a smile. I used to do that as well.

"Why are you a commie?" Greg asked suddenly. "And into Crowley! Aren't they, like, opposites?"

"Yes, they are opposites," I said. "But they have a lot in common. It's all about changing consciousness, and creating a kind of personal discipline that can change the world." We were cutting across a lawn, breaking every rule of suburbia, just like every kid ever did all the time.

"But, fucking Satan . . ."

"Karl Marx occasionally signed his letters 'Old Nick.' He knew what he was doing."

"Satan doesn't believe in equality!" Greg blurted out. A treeful of birds took flight. "Communism is all about the weak conquering the strong. The strong should rule!"

"Shucks, Greggie. Did you buy a copy of *The Satanic Bible* at the B. Dalton in the mall with your bar mitzvah money?"

"What, you think it's bullshit?"

"Anything you can buy in a shopping mall is bullshit, dude."

"You can buy *The Communist Manifesto* in a mall too," Greg said.

"No, anything *you* can buy, Greg," I said. "Would you buy *The Communist Manifesto*? Can you? Can you bear to pick up a copy, bring it over to the cashier, and pay five bucks for your very own copy of Marx and Engels?" I didn't look back as I turned the corner around a house where the backyard never ended, but just melded into the wooded area behind Bernstein's shack.

"Well, why would I want to buy—"

"Greg," I said. Using a person's name repeatedly is a powerful way of focusing their attention. "I'll let you *fuck* me if you can buy a copy of the fucking book. I'm not even joking. I'll put your balls in my mouth. I'll do it even if you just *say* you can buy a copy."

Greg snorted. "Communism's fucking over. People are running away from it. They want blue jeans and the Scorpions."

"So, no cock sucking?"

"No."

"Then you, my friend," I said, "have a cop in your head. What are you, a rebel and a tough guy who wants to grind the weak under his heel just because he can, or . . ." I let it hang there. Before Greg could even say his snotty little, "Or *what*?" I added, "A proud American?"

"I am a proud American!" Greg said. He caught himself, blushed again, but too late. "I mean, we're the fucking best. We rock." He added, more quietly, "Fuck you, Dawn."

"Keep America beautiful," I said. "Let's pick up some of this stuff and see what we can see." We were atop the hill over Bernstein's cabin. There was yellow police tape everywhere, but it drooped into puddles and piles of leaves. LILCO, or the county, or whoever was supposed to be in charge, hadn't bothered to remove the tree. Some of Bernstein's papers had escaped through the gash in the roof and were tangled up in the grass, in those fingery autumn branches he loved, or had just dissolved into blue-and-white piles of pulp from exposure to the elements. I did find an old *Love and Rockets* comic I had left there and hugged it to myself. Greg asked, incredulously, "Girls read comics?" I rolled my eyes at him.

Most of the papers were beyond salvaging. The ink had fallen right off the pages—Bernstein was a snob for fountain pens and never typed or printed anything up. Letters to Bernstein were in better shape, but often full of schizophrenic gibberish or plaintive begging for secrets, insights, and money. After a few disappointing minutes, I convinced Greg, wiry as he was, to climb the tree and see if he could drop down through the hole in the roof to get to the file cabinets.

"Wouldn't it be cool if the body was still in there?" he asked as he scaled the slantways trunk. My heart clenched and died, but I said sure. Greg wormed through the tear in the house and was gone for a few minutes. Then he called for me to meet him by the window, the one through which Bernstein could always see me.

"The cops took a lot of stuff, but the bottom drawers of both cabinets were full. I couldn't get them out, but I pulled the folders." Greg handed me a bunch, then ducked down and came up with more. *Wouldn't it be cool if he were trapped in this little gray shack forever, starving and decaying but never dying?* I thought while waiting for him to make his way back up the hole and around the yard, but he managed it anyway. Greg lost interest in the materials right away, when he saw that a lot of it looked like math and much of the rest like train schedules from unknown cities. Indeed, much of it made little more sense to me than 777 did, but I had some understanding of what was being described and discussed. And occulted, of course.

Greg, in his invincible ignorance, noticed something I didn't. "Some of this penmanship is weird," he said. We were sitting against the side of the house, open folders on our laps. "Same pen, right?" He held up two pieces of paper—originals, not carbons. Bernstein had always mailed people carbons but kept his own work close by. Something about art in the age of mechanical reproduction. "Different handwriting. Are any of these yours, maybe? This one looks girly."

It was automatic writing. Correspondence between Bernstein and himself, or his Holy Guardian Angel. It looked almost like but not exactly like his usual penmanship. I took the folder from Greg and started skimming. Greg was attracted to these letters because they were actual letters—a Platonic dialogue of sorts, almost comprehensible to someone like him. Bernstein had had a crisis of "faith," for lack of a better word, when people started leaving the Eastern bloc en masse. Bernstein had been a Trotskyist years ago, and even stood around the Long Island Rail Road yards in Queens with a copy of a mimeographed revolutionary newspaper for a few hours every Thursday evening and Saturday morning, hoping to stir up the proletariat. I'd seen an old copy of the rag—it was mostly concerned with sectarian battles against the "Pabloites," to name something that no LIRR employee was at all concerned with. Bernstein's international had nine members in New York, three in Chicago, and two in Montreal. It was really an extended family; the Canadians were some

cousins of the group's leader, and his wife and kid were
heavily involved as well. But it's the nature of Trotskyist
groups to fission, Bernstein told me, and eventually he found
himself a faction of one after the relatives had some horri-
fying Christmastime argument about El Salvador. Also, half
the New York cadre were FBI agents.

But Bernstein kept at it. Trotskyism was a pure kind of
"antinomian praxis," he explained to his Holy Guardian
Angel—to himself—that had opened many psychic doors.
Even Nazism, that great bellow of rage and resentment from
the disaffected, one that had disguised itself as a manifesta-
tion of the Overman, was disqualified for actually having
had succeeded for a little while. Nothing supported by that
many frumpy hausfraus could truly be a rebellion—Bernstein
could be a sexist, like all men, regardless of their politics. Of
course, Bernstein was also Jewish, which made the cultiva-
tion of Nazi politics problematic. Would anyone at the
American Nazi Party ever even write him back? But
Trotskyism—there was a political framework that wouldn't
ever win. But now, that was Bernstein's problem. Not only
was Trotskyism not winning politically; it wasn't winning
intellectually. None of Trotsky's predictions had come true.
They were all unraveling, every night on television. Soon
there would be no alternative to neoliberal capitalism at all.
*O Holy Guardian Angel, what shall I do?*

The response wasn't *Shoot yourself in the head, boychik.*

Then Greg said, "Hey, do you think it's true what they say:
the perpetrator always returns to the scene of the crime?"

"People say that?"

"On television, they do. But even then it's . . ."

"Ironic? A cliché that they're making fun of."

Greg said, "Yeah. But where did the idea come from? Is it
true?"

"Are you worried?" I asked. "Maybe he already came and left."

"Maybe *he's* here right now," Greg said. "Or *she*."

"Oh, you think it was me. I see. I thought you were confessing at first." Greg was getting agitated. The best thing to do with an agitated moron is to fan the flames, so they do something exceptionally stupid.

"Maybe it was you. Maybe you're trying to frame me. We're interfering with a crime scene, aren't we? God, this was fucking stupid—" He threw down the papers he had been leafing through. "Is this evidence? Are my fingerprints on this evidence now? Holy shit, Dawn, what the fuck are you doing to me?"

I turned square to look at him, fill his vision. "What are we doing here, Greg? Why did you come with me?"

"Look, I . . . You owe me."

"Oh, I owe?" I laughed. "Oh I oh hi-ho!" Greg needed to know I was laughing at him. The big black thing roared up from the Abyss living under where our asses sat and filled my body, swimming behind my eyes. "What do I owe you, eh?"

"Fuckin' bitch." He licked his lips. His eyes got wide. He didn't have the Will for what he wanted to do to me—a slap across the face, followed by some bullshit HBO movie love rape—but he was close.

"C'mere," I told him, and slid my hand around his head to pull him close. We kissed. I slid onto his lap, then I bit his face, hard, tearing into the flesh of his lips and cheeks. He shrieked and pushed me away. Greg was a skinny guy, but boys have good upper body strength. That's what I was expecting, of course, so when he pushed me off of him, I took the skin between my teeth with me. He covered up, curled into a ball, and howled. I spit out what was in my mouth and scrambled to my feet, ready to kick in his ribs if he found some courage and came at me. But Greg had nothing but a faceful of pain that wouldn't go away. The flesh around the mouth is full of nerves, and germs, but I made sure not to bite him so hard that he'd lose consciousness or go numb. He needed every moment, and every moment needed to stretch.

"There's some Satan for you, asshole!" I said. "That's what I owed you. So forget about going to the police or your parents or anything. Anyone asks you, you were bitten by a wild dog. Anyone asks me, you tried to rape me and I defended myself. Then your ugly face gets in all the papers, and your parents get to pay for an AIDS test for me. I have use for you, so here's what I'm going to do—I'm going to rush to the very next house and beg them to call an ambulance. And you'll get some stitches and you'll be okay. Enjoy the rabies shots, by the way. I'm told it's only seven long needles now, not forty shots in the belly like it used to be."

Then I ran, like I said I would, and called back over my shoulder, "Leave the painting behind the shed in your yard. I'll pick it up later!"

# 6.

Bernstein had promised me that he would do something that worked. I'd challenged him in the ways I now know are typical of idiot seekers. "If you're such a powerful magician, how come you're not rich?" I demanded to know, though most of my spending money came from him, and I certainly had never seen him put on a suit and go to work for it. Like the fancy old ladies who never bought hats, but just *had* them, Bernstein always just had whatever amount of money he needed. He just laughed and told me that most Marxists who take it seriously—"and who aren't in a political cult"—end up rich sooner or later. "We understand capitalism so much better than anyone else, after all."

"All right. Can you make people do things they wouldn't normally do?" I asked, from between his pasty thighs. I didn't even make eye contact with him when I sucked him off, because he didn't like that. His leg hair tickled me. But it doesn't take magick to be richer than a high school kid, or to get a girl to suck a dick. Crowley's definition—*Magic is the Science and Art of causing change to occur in accordance with the Will*—sounded to me like a cop-out, and I said as much. Any eight-year-old learning to play the piano is a magician, then.

Bernstein nodded, and *hrmmed* sonorously. I suppose chatting during cock-sucking breaks was my way of establishing some independence. "Many people would now feed you a line about quantum entanglement or some other scientific theory they don't understand. I certainly don't understand quantum mechanics, or any more physics than it takes to ride a teeter-totter successfully or set a kettle of tea to boil.

"But I am a materialist, Amaranth." He still occasionally called me Amaranth, which always felt like a subtle bit of mockery and affection simultaneously. "The world is matter in motion and nothing else. The mystic sees the world as an illusion—but the magician must see reality square in the face." He tapped me on the shoulder. I could stop tonguing his balls, I guessed.

"If you want to see something real, come with me," he said. He pulled up his pants and went to the small wardrobe next to the television. A few minutes later we were out back. He had turned off the lights and the television, and we were far enough from both the other houses and the road that the woods were dark. Bernstein had thrown on a churchy-looking robe and held a thin lance in his hand. He drew a circle around us, then another, then made some marks in the dirt. It was too dark to see, and a bit chilly. I was neither an enthusiast nor was I a skeptic; I was just a disinterested party, watching some intriguing ritual, as I did virtually every evening anyway. Bernstein said some words, and snapped the lance in half over his knee. Then we waited.

I waited for my eyes to adjust, but they didn't. I thought about something I'd learned in my psychology elective. It's very difficult to determine if hypnosis actually "works" to make people do things that are unsafe or that go against their natures. Most subjects under hypnosis will drink what they're told is a vial of acid. So too will people who aren't under hypnosis, as long as they're part of a hypnosis experiment. So I was awake and even agitated in my own brain, the little homunculus with his hands on the levers of my limbs waiting for the signal to run, or to punch Bernstein, or to just keep them shivering and twitching ever so slightly. So, was I being hypnotized, or was I just a part of a hypnosis experiment?

I reached forward to find Bernstein and instead hit stone. A great slab wall of the smoothest stone, and I knew there was no wall like that around, knew that I hadn't lost any time so couldn't have been shoved into a car and transported somewhere. I touched my own face to make sure I hadn't been blindfolded—and to make sure I wouldn't feel stone no matter what I came into contact with—and my face was fine. I took a step back and bumped into another wall. I spread both arms and hit a wall with one, then the other. It was a pentagon, five walls all around me, with rounded corners. The floor was still dirt and leaves and twigs, but I dug with my hands at the base and found only wall. I took a pebble light enough that it wouldn't kill me coming back down and threw it high to look for a ceiling, or a rim. It landed right in front of me without hitting anything. I remembered the steel toes in my boots, braced myself, and kicked the wall in front of me. It was solid; I felt the impact in my shin. I shouted for Bernstein and my voice sounded like I was at the bottom of a well. Was this a real thing? Had I been led into a well somehow? And now, Bernstein would take my skin off with a potato peeler and wear it himself.

Bernstein stepped in front of me and snapped his fingers, setting off some flash paper. That trick I knew, but I blinked hard and reached out blindly to grab his robe. I got it, and started slapping at him. "What the fuck! What the fuck was that!"

"Magick!" Bernstein took the blows easily enough. My heart wasn't really in them anyway.

"How did you do that?" Finally, my eyes adjusted to the dazzle and the dark and I could see him.

"As I said . . . magick."

"Was there something under the robe?" I reached for it, but he pulled away. "Did you smear LSD on your cock?"

"That would be intriguing for both of us, what with the glans being mucocutaneous tissue," he said brightly.

I sputtered as I realized what I was saying, but I couldn't think of many other rational explanations. Bernstein snickered, and then shrugged. "I can't tell you how I did it, or even what I did. I can show you. It will take a long time. You'll have to do what I say without question or hesitation. Much of what I will ask of you will seem incomprehensible, stupid, or contradictory. And—"

"And in the end, when I'm ready to hear the big secret, to learn the Key to It All, you'll whisper in my ear, 'The secret is that there is no secret,'" I said.

"That, I swear I won't do, Amaranth." Bernstein even put his hand over his heart. "There are a lot of tricksters and frauds, but I am not one of them. In fact, I'm pretty much the only not-one of them. What you experienced was magick. I'm happy to initiate you into the practice. Now, let's go back inside."

I was tempted to leave, but I had left my bag inside. And inside, I saw something far more real. It was a tiny man, about two feet tall, with a furry ass and legs. A *satyr*—my mind groped for the word. He smiled at me, showing off a face full of shark's teeth, then he leapt through the window, shattering it. I fell to my knees. The room smelled like raw meat and composting summertime grasses. I had a million questions, but I knew there'd be no answers.

Even now, I still have theories. Hallucinogens and hypnosis, plus a BB gun. A balloon or a puppet or a midget confederate for some long con or sex game that Bernstein would have completed had he not been shot in the head. I've read all the

Houdini stuff, the Amazing Randi material, the endless debunkings. I know prestidigitation and the various tricks, just like any twelve-year-old with a library card might. And I know how even in its debased and tawdry form, stage magic honors the real thing.

# 7.

I learned. In my own primitive way, I'd made Greg an acolyte. Marked him in a way that separated him from the world he knew, and brought him into my world. Had he been smarter, I would have had to have been cleverer. But he wasn't that bright, just bright enough to make an okay ally, and likely a perfect fall guy if needed. A few years ago, in Northport, a longhair acidhead named Ricky Kasso killed some guy who owed him money. Then he killed himself. Kasso had played his murder up with all the minor-league spectacle he could muster—he brought the guy out to the woods, shouted, "Say you love Satan!" and even scrawled SATAN LIVES on a nearby boulder. Or he tried to anyway. Ricky Kasso wasn't very smart either, so he spelled it SATIN LIVES. He wasnvt even into partic-ularly dark metal. He liked AC/DC and Judas Priest, to name two bands that get played on WBAB thirty times a day. There's nothing to that music, either forward or backward. If there were, everyone in high school would already be dead. But it upsets parents and it upsets cops, so longhairs are practically the niggers of the North Shore now. Greg would make a great lightning rod, if necessary.

Greg didn't look too bad, even with the stitches in his lips and on his cheek. I could see the outline of my mouth, just like after the first bite of a sandwich, but to his school friends it probably looked totally badass. He had brought me the painting.

"How did you know where I lived?"

"Small town," he said. "Your grandma is in the book, and everyone knows about your father." His voice was muffled a bit by the fact that his lip was stapled together. I smiled and let him in.

"It's totally cool that you're here. Do you want to meet my grandmother? She loves company. I can just wake her from her nap." I said that just to get him to leave. Then Grandma appeared in the doorway between the living room and kitchen. There were toast crumbs all over her chin and house-dress. She smiled, unashamed.

"Hello," she said to Greg. She glanced down at the painting. "That's a painting of fire. Fire so hot buildings wilt. Did you paint it?" Then she added, "What happened to your face, young man? Was it a terrible wolf in the woods?"

"He painted it for me!" I said. I took a hold of Greg's elbow and started tugging him toward my room. "Grandma, *General Hospital* is on. Do you need help with the TV?"

"Naw," she said. "I got it." She always knew exactly where the remote control was.

"Room's a mess, sorry," I told Greg. The usual sort of thing—clothes on the floor, books open and spine up like banana peels thrown over someone's shoulder, a desk crowded with Bernstein's papers and some of my own doodles and work. No place to sit but the bed and the desk chair. Greg chose the bed immediately. I took the chair and sat in it backwards, legs spread on either side of its back, like a boy.

"Tough guy, eh?" I said. Then in an impression of his voice, half my mouth stuck together, "*I know where you live.*"

"You think you can fuck me up like you did and get away with it?" Greg said.

"Yes, yes I do." He didn't say anything to that and made no move, so I explained the whole thing to him. "I've already gotten away with it. You kick my ass, kill my grandmother, rape me, burn this whole apartment complex down, I'll have already gotten away with it. Whatever little consequences you think you can introduce into my life are irrelevant. I'm not into revenge. I'm not into ju—" I stopped myself, but it was the thought that counted, so I snatched a pen from my desk, lifted my shirt, grabbed a bit of flab with my free hand and jabbed it in, hard as I could. "Fuck!"

Greg was taken aback. "Holy shit. Look at your fucking stomach."

"That's some real magick," I told him. "But I'm still trying to get it right." He put his hand to his face. Grandma cracked the door open then and asked what was wrong. Not because she'd heard my cry or was concerned, or even remembered that I was in my room with a strange and wounded boy, but because there was a commercial on the television and she came to check me out five times an hour on schedule. Greg was startled. I took the opportunity to slide off the chair and slip into his blind spot. Grandma wandered off, as she does, and I sniffed Greg's hair. He jumped back and threw a wild arm at me but I ducked.

"Okay . . . Jesus, fuck," he said. "That was impressive and weird. How did you get so close to me without me even knowing? Did you plan that with your grandmother?"

I held up the bloody pen. "Want to learn how? This time, you'll have to make your own wound."

"Can I have a different pen? You know, AIDS. I mean not that you have AIDS."

"There's a razor in the bathroom. With a pink handle," I said.

Greg, his left palm wrapped in a rag made from one of my father's old T-shirts, had some good ideas, and made a list of them. Suspects. Means, motive, and opportunity. Ratiocination. But not individuals—we had no way of collecting clues from the scene, no neighborhood to canvas, and when magick was involved, means could *mean* anything. He had boiled it down to some groups: rival occultists, or a possible other "acolyte" who had been jealous of me. Rival Communists—Trotskyist, Stalinist, Maoist, or even anarcho-terrorist. The ruling class. The middle class. Organized crime. Or some combination thereof. Sounded like a long list, but except for the middle class, there were very few folks fitting the bill on Long Island, and of the remainder very few who knew who Bernstein was. Virtually all his acquaintances and correspondents might have had a reason to kill him, occult or otherwise.

"Why wouldn't a magician just kill him with magic?" Greg said. He took up a pencil and made to temporarily scratch out "rival occultists" from his list, which was blue streaked with red thanks to my bloody pen.

"It's not that easy to do something with *just* magick," I said.

"Do you know where to begin looking for other magicians?"

"No," I had to admit. And the idea of Bernstein maybe having another initiate out there, one who took him out, was especially upsetting. I pushed it out of my mind. "So, political rivals? That should be easy. Nobody mainstream gives a shit about Marxism anymore, not even as an enemy, what with glasnost and all the shit happening in East Germany these days."

"So, Nazis and commies," Greg said. There was one place to look. I snatched a flier from my desk and told Greg to wait in the bedroom. In the kitchen, I picked up the phone and called the hardcore show hotline. It was an answering machine tape recorded by some guy out from Queens, or at least someone from Queens. His accent, all lispy and nasal as though mixing Brooklyn, Long Island, and the sounds of

mental retardation, gave it away. He never gave a name, and
was entirely nonpartisan. Far-right bullshit punk shows held
in some asshole's basement or a Polish American hall—Nazis
liked playing in the clubs of their former victims, of course
disguising their intentions to gain power—were listed alongside real house shows, club gigs, and college events. There
was something going on virtually every night, and all of it
invisible to anyone not already in the know. Hardcore was a
lot like magick: ritual, rage, and rebellion. Something that
most people knew nothing about or were terrified by. Some
marginal few discovered, embraced, and were consumed by
it. A few brave folks even made it out alive at the other end.

There was a show tonight, in a basement on Woodhull
Avenue. A few years ago, that was just a road through a wood
connecting a development to Nesconset Highway, but now it
had about a dozen identical houses and even a shitty little
strip mall with a deli and a locksmiths' anchoring it. Not a
good place for a show, but the band had an intriguing name:
Abyssal Eyeballs. A reference to Nietzsche's old saw about
staring into the abyss until the abyss stares back, probably.
But that could be a Nazi group, or an anti-Nazi group. Or
some art fags who liked silly names and found abyssal
eyeballs euphonious and obnoxious in equal proportions, as
I did. At any rate, it was a show and five bucks, nobody turned
away.

Greg had to call his mom to get permission to go. "This is
your fault," he hissed at me, pointing at his injury. "I used to
be able to go wherever the fuck I wanted."

"Pfft, you don't even have a car."

Anyway, permission was granted thanks to his mother's
answering the phone through a haze of Valium and we had
some time to kill, so I made him, and Grandma, some grilled
cheese sandwiches and tomato soup. I giggled at myself the

entire time. Greg even struck up a conversation with Grandma about life on Long Island. Her father, my great-grandfather, was a German immigrant to Brooklyn who wanted a life for his family away from the grime and crime of the big city, so he looked in the newspaper and found a cheap house in Port Washington. But he got his presidents wrong and got on the LIRR to Port Jefferson. Great-Grandpa was very confused when he got here and asked the ticket agent for help. "Well, you can go all the way back to Jamaica, and then get on the train to Port Washington," the ticket agent had said. "Or I can show you my house. I happen to be selling it." And that was the great two-family Victorian that went to my father after Great-Grandpa died and that we all lived in until my father discovered crack and sold all the furniture and then let the bank foreclose on it. Grandma didn't mention that part. Grandma and Greg even watched an episode of *Wheel of Fortune* together, while I flipped through some of the materials we had salvaged from Bernstein's files. Every so often she'd turn to him and ask, "Oh Lord, what happened to your face!" He'd say, "A dog bit me," and she'd mention her friend from grade school whose leg was nearly torn off by a wild dog back in Brooklyn.

"Greg and I are going out, Grandma," I told her finally, and her face lit up.

"Oh, wonderful!" she said. "Well, do have a good time."

"Uh, bye, Mrs. . . ." Greg said. Grandma didn't offer up her surname, perhaps having forgotten it, so I said, "Seliger," and Greg repeated it and Grandma told him to call her Helen.

"You should," I said when we were out the door. "Helen is her name." But he didn't laugh.

It wasn't a long walk, but it was getting dark earlier now that the fall had come. A few plastic jack-o'-lanterns in the windows and on the porches of the homes on either side of the street leered at us. I was glad to have grabbed the big cop flashlight from atop Grandma's fridge to light our way.

"How are you going to explain the gash on your hand to your mom?"

"I'm not," Greg said. "Don't need to. She won't notice. My face was hard to hide, the palm easy to hide."

"Ah, hiding in plain sight. Very occult!"

Greg changed the subject. "What kind of show is this? Punk?"

"Probably."

"Fucking punk—so ridiculous."

"What's your problem?"

"There's no virtuosity," Greg said. "Punk is just picking up an instrument and slamming against it like an idiot. Can any of the bands on your jacket play a real lick? Read music? Do they even fucking practice?"

"That's the point, though. It's something anyone can do—" I started to say.

"I get the point. The point is bullshit. People lump in punk and metal just because they're both loud and use power chords, but metal has more in common with Vivaldi. It's real music. I listen to anything, so long as there's some excellent musicianship, and I'm treated like I eat shit for breakfast every morning. Have you ever even heard of Jaco Pastorius?" He pantomimed a bass and did that doob-de-doob-moob thing with his mouth that bassists do when trying to impress women.

"Can't say that I have. Maybe you'll play him for me some-time."

He muttered something about yeah, maybe, and we were there. The site of the show was a nondescript house. Actually, the house was so nondescript that I instantly thought it was some sort of trap. It looked like the sort of thing a little kid might draw if you handed her some crayons and said, "Draw a house." A door with a single step before it, one window on either side, perfectly clean siding and brown shingles. Even a chimney, but one coming out of the room rather than built alongside an exterior wall.

"You knock," I said.

"You knock," Greg said. "My hand hurts."

So I knocked, and a young Hispanic man answered. Nobody I'd seen around before, though I go to house shows all the time. He didn't seem shocked to see a girl with a bright orange Mohawk and a big spiked leather jacket at his door so I asked if there was a show.

"In the basement, yeah. Go around back. There's a cellar door. I was about to put up a sign." He held up a sign with a big red arrow on it, smacked it onto the door, then closed it on us.

"That must be an example of the friendly punk rock community, eh?" Greg said. "And that arrow will really be helpful. People won't just walk down the block, even if they knew what to make of it."

"You can go home if you want," I said, but he was right. There was something queer going on, but it's not as though I had any other leads. And there was something about an imminent experience, the unknown about to become known, that twisted my stomach into delicious knots. It's why I did anything I did, really, from taking a set of clippers to my hair to climbing a tree and looking into a bedroom window, half hoping I'd be caught. I had to see who, and what, was in the basement. My Will was strong, Greg's not so much, so he followed. There was a cellar door, it was open, and from it spilled the low murmurs of conversation.

The basement was spotless. Not even spotless in the lived-in rumpus room way. Like the house above, everything looked brand new—the clean boiler, the blank gray walls, the freshly poured cement floor, the unfinished wooden staircase in the corner leading back upstairs to, I presumed, the empty living room and static-charged wall-to-wall carpet. The basement was so pristine that it looked empty even though about a dozen people were already present, clumped in twos and threes. Nobody turned to greet us, or even look at us. And I recognized nobody. This wasn't the usual crowd. One girl had a Chelsea haircut with a pretty pronounced curl, looking more like a mostly bald Bob's Big Boy than was good for her, but most of the others weren't even punks. The great big graduate student from my route, and his tiny girlfriend, were in one corner. I wanted to rush up to him and say, "Aram, hello!" but of course he'd have no idea who I was. But then I realized—that's exactly what I should do, especially as Greg was getting antsy and twitchy standing next to me and waiting for something to happen.

"Aram, hello!" I said as I walked on up to him, my hand out like a used car salesman. "And Karen."

Aram smiled and shook my hand. "Hello, how are you?" he said, his face exploding with a real, authentic smile. Karen looked confused and wilted. Clearly, she should be paired off with Greg, and I should have had Aram. We both decided to play friends.

"So, Abyssal Eyeballs!" I said. "Haven't seen them before!"

"Me neither. It should be . . ." Aram said, glancing around the room. His hair nearly scraped against the low ceiling. "An interesting show."

"My name is Karen," Karen finally said.

"Dawn, and this is Greg."

Greg mumbled a hello. Then he said, "Where's the instruments?"

"It's not a musical," Karen said. "It's a straight play."

"More performance art, actually," Aram said. "I'm pretty sure there will be instruments."

"See, performance art," I said to Greg, nudging him with my elbow. "With instruments."

"What happened to your face?" Karen asked him.

"Pit bull with AIDS," Greg said with a laugh. Wrong crowd for bumper sticker humor. Nobody found his joke funny, but everyone in the basement quieted down and turned to look at him. Or past him, as the lights overhead dimmed and the door to the upstairs opened, yellow and orange light, and fog-machine fog spilling out onto the staircase. The cellar door through which we had entered slammed shut behind us.

Karen was wrong—there were instruments. Two surpetis sounded from somewhere in the room, droning on at tones so slightly different as to almost create a third, weird buzz. A strobe started. Someone had a violin. Most of the people around us weren't waiting for a band; they were part of a show. Aram and Karen, and the Chelsea girl, appeared to be spectators, but that was it. One man had glow-in-the-dark face paint. Then things got a little weird.

"If I do not throw a physical bomb, it is only because there is none big enough . . . There can be no peace between Socrates and Athens, between Jesus and Jerusalem. We must then first throw moral bombs!" someone bellowed. It was a line from Crowley's *The World's Tragedy*. A guitar started grinding away, more black metal than hardcore. The surpetis droned endlessly. Other members of the band—the cast?— started taking off their clothes. Greg was making out with the Chelsea girl, or seemed to be as best I could determine in the momentary flashes of light. We'd gone looking for politics, but found some sort of vaguely occult performance. I suppose that was to be expected.

"Ladies and gentlemen," said another voice. It was the Latin kid, but far away and tinny. It took me a second to figure out that he was still upstairs and speaking into some kind of vent or pipe that led into the basement. "The Abyssal Eyeballs." The strobe slowed down. Three people descended from the steps leading to the upstairs. One of them was under a sheet with three circles over the head, like a cartoon ghost. The other two were a slightly overweight woman in sweatpants and facial mud, the other man dressed as though he should have been much older—high pants, a straw hat, black socks, and sandals. As if we already didn't know that suburbia was a soul-raping nightmare. If the ghost was supposed to be the soul of either an abortion or some kid who committed suicide, I was going to leave. But it wasn't. The guitar changed up a bit, the woman started doing some human beatboxing, and the ghost raised its arms under the sheet and twirled like a dervish. It was a woman too, a real dancer. The man began to sing. I heard Aram say aloud to Karen, "This is supposed to be a straight play?" but then I wondered if they too weren't actually part of the show rather than just spectators. Much of the song made no sense to me, as most of the lyrics weren't in English. Each line seemed to be in a different language. Only the old saw from Nietzsche, "Whatever is done from love always occurs beyond good and evil," was in English. I'd taken French in school, but the vocabulary of the lyric in that language was beyond me. Someone handed the ghost woman a guitar. She draped the sheet over her arms to play. The Chelsea girl shouldered past me, tugging Greg behind her. They started pogoing in front of the band. The woman in the mud mask had a bongo drum. The Abyssal Eyeballs got some pretty solid riffing going. I took a deep breath, found a shadow, and got up the steps unmissed.

The kitchen was bare. I noticed that the fridge wasn't humming, and opened it. No light, no power. And the food was all props, like they have in Sears. A big plastic turkey with little plastic trimmings. Empty no-brand juices and sodas. Even fake bread, actually sliced. A pair of plastic fried eggs, with big yellow staring yolks. The living room had no furniture either except for a tall lamp in the corner. Of course, no vent. There were two doors—one was likely a closet, the other perhaps a bedroom. I inhaled, didn't think, grabbed a doorknob, and opened it. A bedroom, yes, with a cot and the Latin kid on it, a small desk lamp on the floor, and some random junk—an easel, paint tubes, a pile of towels, a bass drum and a floor tom, some cardboard boxes likely filled with stuff.

"What?"

"What's with that show downstairs?"

"Don't like it? We're in progress. Making changes. You can leave feedback afterwards, but I have to say I won't take it very seriously if you've already left to come look for me," the kid says. His voice sounded a bit hollow, as though he was still speaking into the vent.

"I mean, what is this supposed to be about?" I was angry, annoyed, asking all the wrong questions. I felt like some Long Island idiot wandering the halls of MOMA and snorting derisively at the artwork. *My kid could paint that!* "I mean, what's your name? Are you new in town?" Below my feet, the band in the basement thumped like the building's very own heart.

The kid smiled. "You meant to ask me my name, but instead you accidentally asked me to explain to you the themes of the Abyssal Eyeballs. Honestly, I don't even know. This just felt like something I had to do. It's, like, important somehow."

"Let's pretend that is so," I said.

"My name is Roderick."

"Do you live here?" He looked around the room, eyes questioning. "Yes, I mean in this house?"

"Of course not."

"New in town?"

"You forgot to preface that with 'Hey, sailor,'" he said. That made the blood rush to my head. My Will was totally scattered. His was quite focused. "Anyway, I have to do something now," he said, reaching for some papers on the cot. Then he leaned down near the vent in the wall and put his hand on the lever to open it. "Please close the door behind you. Help yourself to anything you might find in the fridge. And promise me you won't do something crazy, like kill yourself and leave blood everywhere, while I'm setting up."

He chuckled, and didn't even look up at me, but I said, "I promise." I stepped out and closed the door. I even went to the fridge, in case he was giving me some sort of clue. Life wasn't like that; there was nothing of interest in the fridge, though it did occur to me that the Abyssal Eyeballs were squatting here—maybe for the night, maybe forever. I could go down to the deli and call the police on the pay phone to shake things up. But cops can ruin things, and I was no rat, plus the notion smacked of spite, of flipping over a chessboard. From the small kitchen window I saw the backyard filling with people. The show was already over. Greg and the Chelsea girl were holding hands. I decided on a disappearing act.

**8.**

I've been a punk for three years. My initial reason was pretty stupid. Once my father started disappearing for a few days at a time, I realized that I wasn't going to have a sweet sixteen party when the time came. The lights went off, and Grandma had to call LILCO to get the power back on. She thought she was growing forgetful, and she was, but paying the bills had always been Mom's gig and she had never let anything slip, until Dad was home one summer after a layoff and decided to take over. Then the phone started ringing off the hook, and the caller on the other line was always asking for her, even after she died. You have to pay for cancer treatments whether they work or not, as it turns out.

Life was getting a lot smaller. People started drifting away from one another, finding their own little sections of the unicursal hexagram back when I was thirteen, when Mom was still alive, when I was spending a lot of time at the hospital. Then Dad started acting oddly, and as news travels fast in a small town the good girls started keeping me at arm's length. The bad girls didn't give a fuck about me either. And guys—it was either play Dungeons & Dragons, or spread my legs. Neither option was all that appetizing. So I spent a lot of time in my room, compulsively rereading the few books I owned: *Anne of Green Gables*, and *Been Down So Long It Looks Like Up to Me*, which I'd liberated from Dad, were special favorites.

One night I was fiddling with the radio and turned the knob almost all the way to the left of the dial. Someone on TV had said that classical music helps with relaxation, but instead I got an ear-raping roar of guitars and vocals that sounded like barking. It was WUSB, the local college station, and the program was Outrage, a hardcore punk show. For what seemed like a very long while, I didn't move. My hand stayed on the knob. I don't remember breathing, but I must have, because a dozen songs later, when the DJ's voice came on to read off the names of the songs, and the bands, and where they were from—England! California! Mexico! *Long Island!*—I exhaled so completely I nearly fainted. I'd never heard of any of the bands, but rushed for a pencil and paper to write down some names.

The show was two hours long, and I'd missed some of it, but I spent at least ninety minutes practically wrapped around the radio. Critics and parents say that hardcore is just noise, and honestly, they're right. On that first night, and for many Wednesday nights thereafter, I could hardly tell one song from another, and the DJ never repeated a song. I wrote down snippets of lyrics I could comprehend and even attempted to transcribe riffs that I liked, scribbling down brbrbrbrbrbrbrrrrreeeeng and the like. It was a whole new secret world, populated mostly by guys, doing things all by themselves. They were bored and disgusted, just as I was, so they created their own little kingdom with its own aesthetics, politics, and foreign policy. An aggressive, expansionist foreign policy aimed at colonizing the suburbs where I lived. By the end of the month, I was a dedicated fifth columnist.

The weeks between Wednesdays dragged on. That's when I took up my hobby of peering in through windows to see how the other ninety-nine percent lived. I suppose I was trying to find a new way to live, or at least a happy family that I could pretend to be a part of. That, and I wanted to get caught doing it, so that my father would wake up, so that some kindly social worker or teacher would take an interest in me. But I was already invisible. One night, instead of listening to Outrage, I decided to try to meet the DJ, whom I imagined to be a boy maybe just a year or two older than me, with a great cockscomb of a Mohawk and long muscular arms. A thin guy, tall too. So I took the bus to Stony Brook, as on-campus parking is terrible, found the student union, and for about an hour before the show started, hovered around outside the door to the station.

WUSB's studio was on the far side of the corner of the student union, so there was little traffic in the hallway. I didn't attract much attention. I didn't even bring a book to read, or a snack, and spent about forty-five minutes silently fuming at myself, my stomach enflamed and squirming, should-I-stay-or-should-I-go arguments won and lost every second. Finally, with a grunt, a man carrying a milk crate full of records turned the corner and walked past me. I got a look at one of the covers, and it was nothing like hardcore. He hit the buzzer with his elbow, and said, "Trevor, let me in." Trevor was the name of the hardcore DJ—he must have already been in the studio preparing for the show, even before I got there. And there was Trevor's voice, tinny and distant, saying, "Okay," then the door buzzed, and the man shouldered open the door and let it swing shut behind him.

I took a deep breath, and pressed the buzzer. I heard Trevor's voice saying, "WUSB?" impatient and questioning at once, and then I ran from him like a fool.

"What is the sound of one class struggling?" a guy behind a card table asked me as I tried to hustle out of the student union. There were a number of student clubs out that afternoon. Some Hindu cult with a diorama of a lion about to attack a sheep with a man's face, a number of ethnic clubs and frats, and this guy, who didn't look like a student. A perennial graduate student, maybe. He was tall, even in his chair, with glasses, and balder than any teacher in my high school. If there was anyone else in his club, they weren't tabling with him. A sign taped to the edge of the table read RED SUBMARINE in handwritten black swirls and a number of zine-like pamphlets decorated the tabletop. They were all homebrew jobs.

He handed me one entitled *The Tao of Marxism* and said, "Interested in overthrowing society?"

"Well, which society?"

"What you got?" he asked, and laughed.

"I'm not a student here. I go . . . somewhere else."

"It's okay. We do work in the community too. And in our minds." He tapped the pamphlet he'd given me with one thick finger. "The old revolutionary methods don't work anymore. I mean, look at the Soviet Union, at China." At the time, I knew almost nothing about either country, except that they had nuclear weapons and were "bad" and the people were poor and had to stand in long lines for toilet paper in Russia, and rice in China. "They're just the other side of the coin." He leaned in close. I took a step back. We had opposite ends of the pamphlet pinched between our fingers. "What's your major?" he asked me.

"Uh . . . psychology?" I blushed hard. I certainly didn't feel like a college freshman. I wanted to run again, but there were so many eyes on me, or there seemed to be anyway. And I did want the pamphlet. "But I have to go now. Can I just take this . . . ?" I tried to pluck the zine away from him, but he had a well-practiced grip.

"It's a dollar," he said. "It's a Red Submarine pamphlet I wrote. Not to be confused with any other organization on campus, or anywhere on earth with a similar name, like Red Bal—" He stopped himself, probably because my eyes were rolling to the back of my head, caught his breath, and started again. "I'm Mike Schmidt, the leader of Red Submarine."

"Mike Schmidt—like the baseball player?"

"Yup! Iron Mike. I actually love the Phillies," Mike Schmidt said, suddenly happy. "Are you into baseball?"

I dug up a crumpled dollar from the pocket of my jeans. Bus fare, plus if I bought his shit I wouldn't have to talk about baseball. I'd have to take the train home and hope that either the conductor didn't bother to check for new passengers between Stony Brook and Port Jefferson or hide in the lavatory the entire trip. "Wait, is paying for things properly Communist?"

Mike let go of the pamphlet and smiled a big toothy smile. "Excellent question!" Then he snatched the money from my hand anyway. "The answer might be in the pamphlet, which is now yours to read."

"So . . . are there even any other members in Red Submarine?"

Mike shrugged. "Sure. We keep the group small, though, to avoid splits and purges. You know, arguments over political questions and disagreements often lead to organizations breaking apart."

"So you keep yourself a small group on purpose, to not break apart?"

"That's *reverse* psychology," he said.

"Well, then, if I find the pamphlet persuasive, I certainly won't come back and join your group." I was pleased with myself for that little rejoinder. Generally, I wasn't very good at thinking on my feet back then.

"You have leadership potential," Mike said.

"How did you become the leader of your group?"

"By founding it," he said, a little abrupt now.

"Just like in China and Russia, then?" I asked, and he frowned. I'd gone a little too far with the teasing, and was growing embarrassed again. I wasn't here to meet this weirdo, and the guy I wanted to meet was behind a closed door, and his show was about to start. My Walkman had an FM tuner, so I put my headphones on, waved the pamphlet like a goodbye, and tried my best to walk away without rushing. There were free copies of the *Village Voice* in the vestibule, and I'd never had access to one before, so grabbed one too.

*The Tao of Marxism*, I understand now, made very little sense. Mike Schmidt was a "freelance revolutionary" and had been since he was a freshman back in the 1960s. The About the Author section was two pages long. The whole pamphlet was only sixteen pages. But in its way it was mind blowing. Mike liked Lenin, which surprised me given his comments on the Soviet Union, and was enthusiastic about what he called "the anarchist Lenin," whom he found hiding between the lines of several of Lenin's writings. A lot of the rest of the pamphlet was a rant against traditional leftist organizations—SWP, CP, RCP, RWG, the IS and the ISO, with the ISO being a split from the IS. I was reminded of a microbe budding little O-shaped daughter cells in order to reproduce. Regents-level biology, you know. There were a whole raft of other abbreviations he never deigned to name or even describe. That was all fine and sensible, if poorly written, radicalism, but then there were the last three pages. The revolution wasn't an event that was going to come; it had already happened. There were a couple of million leftists in the US—anarchists and Marxists and Greens, anyone to the left of the Democrats, basically—and they were all doing something in culture, in industry, in schools. One day, they'd all do the same revolutionary thing at the same time, like iron filings influenced by a magnet, and the revolution, already "both imminent and immanent," would be complete. All we had to do was join up, somehow. One didn't even need to be a member of Red Submarine to be a "red submarine," obscured under the waters of capital, ready to act in response to the revolutionary yang impulse to overthrow the yin of reaction. These were the cadre of the Imaginary Party.

It sounded good. Good enough that when I got home and started flipping through the *Village Voice* I decided, on impulse, to shave my head. Plus, maybe then my father would talk to me, and my grandma would say something to me that wasn't about meals or television. I used my father's clippers, and didn't clean it out afterwards. I was ready for an infinity of abuse, and I got it. Kojak and Ban Roll-On jokes from the boys, sneers and outrage from the girls. I shut myself away, piloting a submarine in my own belly, waiting for the revolution.

# 9.

There are almost no girls or women in my life. I had wanted to make friends with that Chelsea girl before she started making out with Greg. After that, I just wanted to talk to her. Bernstein always said that he had almost no other men in his life—in his real life, that is, outside of his busy days writing and responding to letters. We'd found one another thanks to a complex of sociosexual reasons, the demand for yin by yang, and "vice-a-voisa" he had said to me once. Bernstein had a bit of a Queens accent, and years of isolation on Long Island did only a little to dampen it. Only when he was performing a ritual or speaking with his true Will behind him did his voice change, growing deeper, almost senatorial, and the nasal buzz of his voice vanished.

I called WUSB and asked if they had anything by the Abyssal Eyeballs, which was sort of a fool's errand, since their library was so huge. Then I called the concert line, but it was still the same tape from the day before. There were never too many shows on a Tuesday night.

And then I was at loose ends. For years, I'd been wandering from encounter to encounter, from weirdo to weirdo, hunting for other members of the Imaginary Party, my haircut a freak flag which people could salute. I found one in Bernstein, then he was taken from me. I decided to give Grandma another whirl and planted the painting of Crowley's Tower card in front of the television. The apartment was only a one-bedroom, so she slept on a fold-out couch in the living room.

When she awoke, it was slow and awkward, as if each new day was truly a disappointing surprise.

Grandma's eyes focused on the painting, as if it were part of the set of *Good Morning America*. Then she said, "Is it Christmas? Is Jerome coming again?"

"Did he only come on Christmas?" I asked.

"Well, he always came on Christmas," Grandma said. "His parents were Orthodox Jews. He liked the idea of Christmas, I guess, since it was forbidden fruit for him." It had never even occurred to me to think of Bernstein as a human being with parents, possibly siblings, with connections to the world other than the ones he had revealed to me.

"When did you last see him?"

"Oh, oh . . . years ago," she said. "Just before we lost the house."

"Really?" I wanted to reach out and shake her, to crack open her head like an egg and paw through the stupid goop of her brains for the information. "He was at the house?"

"He bought the house . . ." she said. "He was going to let us stay." She sucked on her lip for a moment. "But then he didn't."

"This is Christmas Jerome you're talking about. Jerome Bernstein bought our house when the bank foreclosed?"

"That's right."

"That's fucked." So fucked it was hard to believe. Memories drift like ice floes in the dark sea of Grandma's mind. Sometimes two different ones collide and combine into a new memory of something that never even happened. When Grandma was in her right mind, she hated cursing. Even "shut up" was too much for her. She'd tell me, "Say 'be quiet' if you must say anything, because the word 'quiet' ends with a smile. 'Shut up' ends with a frown." When I turned thirteen I started saying "lighten up" to her in response, but she never

did point out that I was still frowning. She would just frown
and wander away.

Now her antipathy toward cursing was gone. "Oh yes, very
fucked indeed," Grandma said. "That's what put Billy over
the edge, I'm sure."

"Well, why did he?"

"Why did who do what, dear?"

"Why did Jerome buy the house?"

"Oh, Jerome didn't buy our house!" she said.

"Who did?"

"Billy's other friend from school."

"Okay," I said. "Was the name of Billy's other friend from
school . . . Jerome?" Grandma just looked at me. Sometimes
a little presto-changeo like that could help her brain reset,
but not this time.

"No, no," she said. "Jerome is a Jew. This was the other
fellow. Billy's friend from school."

"The non-Jew," I said. "Okay, why did the friend who
wasn't Jewish buy the house?" There had to be an easy way
to find out who owned the house now. The county clerk's
office or something.

Grandma shrugged. "It was going cheap, wasn't it? We'd
been foreclosed on. Billy forgot to pay the mortgage, you see
. . ." Then she forgot what she was going to say. "Let's have
toast with peanut butter this morning," she said, remembering
what she had every morning but not that she had it every
morning.

I didn't have much to actually do, except make Grandma
her breakfast and then do a little laundry. I had no job and
no real desire to get one. If I needed money, I'd think of
something, but my thoughts were scattered and I had
nobody to talk to again. The social world of Long Island
is built around institutions—schools and workplaces.

Without membership in either, there's nowhere to go, nothing to do, except maybe mill around a shopping mall or go downtown.

Downtown had the advantage of being where most of the Hispanics in town lived. Old Raymundo was an exception, probably because he had a high-paying defense job. Maybe I'd run into the Hispanic kid from last night, if my luck held out, and if he even lived in Port Jefferson. He may well have been an invader from Coram.

Port Jefferson's downtown is a "nice place," with the usual mix of dumb little shops: T-shirts, crystals, restaurants that claim that their seafood comes right out of the titular port though it rarely ever does, ice cream and fudge, a mediocre record store and a decent comic book shop, and the excellent Good Read Book Stop off on a side road, away from the day-trippers from Connecticut and the city. The Long Island Rail Road tracks run right through the town, splitting it into the tony Village with its colonial bullshit and its fancy high school, and the tedious Station where I lived and went to school with the heavy-metal dirtbags and unsubtle date rapists. The small Hispanic community tended to be bunched up around the tracks, sprinkled across either side. Of course, he could have been anywhere.

The walk was pleasant except for the usual catcalls and bullshit. I didn't dare wear my headphones. There were too many coincidences swirling about, too many encounters. My Will was diffuse, useless, and I found myself on automatic pilot, heading to the places I usually went to on a stroll. First a peek inside Infant Jesus, where the ex-hippie priest let drug addicts sweep the floors and such for obscure therapeutic reasons. The church and community center were both empty, and the van was gone. Errands, or stolen by a delinquent again? Then I took a left and checked out Barnum Street, which is chock full of nineteenth-century mansions, except for one hideous box with vinyl siding that I absolutely loved because the old Greek widow—her black wardrobe was the tell—with gold teeth kept fifteen cats on the porch and in the weed-choked driveway. Her car wasn't in the drive, and the cats swarmed up to greet me, all tick bitten and one eyeless. I never could hide myself from animals and as Grandma and my father were both allergic to cats, I didn't want to anyway.

Then I cut up through the parking lot and past Rocket Park, which was empty except for a few toddlers and their mothers. Long Island at midday always felt like a neutron bomb hit the place. Most people are gone, but the buildings remain. Rocket Park was so named because of a retrofuturistic and rusted slide shaped like a 1950s missile. The Big One had landed.

I popped into Farpoint Comics, and smiled when all the boys inside gasped. It was an undersmile, really—my lips stayed tight and closed. It was as though my teeth and tongue did the grinning. The "girl in the comic shop" was a role I was long used to, but it never stopped being funny. Nerds were too cowardly to try to pick me up, and almost nobody read *Love and Rockets*. Friggin' *Teenage Mutant Ninja Turtles* was a cartoon now, and everyone knew about indie comics, but the store was still wallpapered with Batman posters and graphic novels of all sorts, and one color—bluish-black—thanks to the movie. Girls were rare as comets around here and twice as hard to communicate with, so nobody bothered to try.

I poked around for a bit, just enjoying the smell of the ink and the way conversations would end as I drifted past, when I saw the flier for yesterday's "event via the Abyssal Eyeballs." That's what the text read, in part.

**BEHOLD!**
**A happening**
**and event**
**via**
**The Abyssal Eyeballs**
**9pm**
**9/18/89**
**(718) 555-6666**

Obviously not the typical punk flier. No stencils, no logos, no hand-scrawled instructions or commentary, and no shadows left behind by photocopying cut-out letters or words. It was laid out on a computer, by a word processing program, and just printed out. And there was a tiny unicursal hexa-gram, and that was some sort of clip art, not hand drawn or cut out either. The number for the venue was the usual concert phone number. But the flier did narrow things down quite a bit—someone with a computer, and probably some money. Not the usual punk rock kid, but I knew that already. More importantly, someone with almost no idea what a proper concert flier should look like. And someone had been here to drop them off.

I took a flier up to the cashier, who was yet another tall fellow in glasses, with bushy hair. "Do you remember this flier?"

"Uhm . . ." he said. He was reading about the friggin' Hulk of all things, but he put down the comic. "I do. There's a whole bunch over there already."

"Yes, I know. Do you remember who dropped these off, or when?"

He smiled. "I thought you had dropped them off, with that guy?" Then he pointed a finger at the top of my head and drew a circle around my hairdo. "But I guess it was someone else."

The Chelsea girl. There are innumerable subtle differences between a Chelsea and a proper Mohawk, but most of them would be invisible to the sort of poor pathetic bastard who'd end up working in a comic book shop in his midthirties. He wasn't even my usual cashier, but I normally came in on Wednesdays anyway.

"And was the guy Spanish?" He just looked at me. "You know, Hispanic? About my age and yay tall. Name of Roderick?" I held a hand over my head. He actually reached out to touch me, and moved my palm about seven inches higher. If he noticed the look on my face—if I could kill someone with my mind, I would have—he didn't register it on his own ugly puss. Then he said, "Nah, an older guy. Big nose. You know . . ." Then sotto voce, "Jewish looking."

"When did this happen?"

"Oh, a few weeks ago," the cashier said. "It was so memorable. To be honest, we don't get a lot of female customers, and they certainly don't come in with older gentlemen. I was sure something kinky was going on."

"I'll be back here soon," I said. "With a picture. Will you be here to identify him as the person you saw?"

"You a cop?" he asked, suddenly suspicious. "I mean, you don't look like a cop." Then he laughed. "What is this, like, *Baker Street* or something?" He meant the comic about a punk Sherlock Holmes that sounded much better than it actually was. His behavior was strange. Never before had a clerk at Farpoint, or any comics shop, not simply fallen all over himself to answer any question I might have.

"Listen, dude, whatever," I told him, and left. I got some ice cream and headed back out to the parking lot. That guy was too husky to walk to work—it was just a matter of figuring out which car was his, and there were few enough in the lot. It was a demographic inevitability that his car would be a piece of shit, and thus I didn't even need to see the NOT ALL WHO WANDER ARE LOST bumper sticker on the off-white 1983 Chevy Chevette to know it belonged to him. And Arby's wrappers littering the well of the front seats; excellent. But most important was the manual lock. So I undid the lace on one of my boots and made a little noose-like loop of it. With the trusty screwdriver on my trusty Swiss Army knife, I pried open the passenger side door the slightest, and then I slid the lace in, snagged the lock, yanked, and popped the door open. Then I moved inside, closed the door, locked it, and ducked under the back seat and waited. The Chevette was a three-door, but I was sure he'd not see me even if he threw a backpack or something in the back before taking off.

This was going to be so much cooler than going to the county clerk's office to find out who owned my old house.

I was tired of being pushed around, of being messed with by virtually everyone I met. Even Greg, even with scars I left decorating his fool mouth, found a way to treat me like shit. I needed to assert my Will once again. The well of the back seat lent itself to yoga and the clearing of the mind, but my thoughts couldn't help but drift toward Bernstein again. Was the Chelsea girl sucking his cock too, and if so, did that make her the killer? My heart rate roared, so I pushed back, toward another memory.

Bernstein once told me what brought him to Mount Sinai. The answer was magick. "This town was once called Old Mans," he said.

"With an apostrophe?" I asked. "Like, belonging to an old man? Or was it some Dutch thing?"

"Depends on the document. It was the eighteenth and nine-teenth centuries after all. Maps were more creative, and perhaps even more accurate for it, back then. When it came time to change the name of the town, the postmaster performed a work of bibliomancy. With a knitting needle in hand, he opened the Bible and felt the hand of God, so he said, draw the point of the needle to the words *Mount Sinai*.

"Names are important things. Your surname, Seliger, means *blessed man*."

"And *Bernstein*?" I asked, because I knew that's what he wanted me to ask. His voice was an octave lower than usual, after all.

"The stone that burns. Amber was thought to be created by burning, but—"

"Sulfur, eh?" I said. Bernstein smiled at me, his little cock-sucking genius. "All fiery and brimstoney. And can the Old Man of Mount Sinai be . . . Saaaatan?" Bernstein normally didn't like my Church Lady impression, but he nodded this time. It was a rare moment of frivolity, and Bernstein's smile was even rarer. I was sufficiently immersed in the memory of it that I barely felt the car move until it stopped in a driveway in Setauket. I scrambled to my feet and before the comic book guy could leave the car I had my shoelace around his neck.

"Surprise!" He was shocked, his eyes wide. I had all the leverage, and his throat, and my Will. I could have killed him then and there, just to show him that I could. To show myself that I could. "Don't piss yourself, please."

He didn't. He glared at me with infinite hate in his rear-view mirror. Who knows how many daydreams of vigilante heroics he had, or fantasies of being tied up by a wanton she-devil of a girl and utterly ravaged? Well, they both had gone right to shit. I tugged a little tighter on the shoelace. "We're going to go inside and have a nice chat."

"I'll . . . fuckin' . . . kill," he said as best he could. True, there was no real way I could get him to let me into his house and chat, but I just wanted him to realize that. I smiled at him and leaned back, planting my knees against the back of his seat. He couldn't get his fat fingers between flesh and rope. He kept eye contact with me, which was good for him, so I could see his eyelids flitter and face go purple. When he was just about to lose consciousness, he suddenly shuddered terribly, and I let him go. My plan had been to leave him in the car, alive, while I checked out his apartment, but I hadn't realized that one of his daydreams was still active. He'd been touching himself through his jeans with his other hand, and had orgasmed. The smell filled the car.

"Holy fuck," I said, and I laughed aloud. "You're totally fucking insane." As I released his throat he started coughing and sputtering. I grabbed the keys from the ignition and left him in the car. My Will guided my fingers around the correct key for the front door on the first try, and I was inside and had the door locked behind me before he even tumbled out of the car and onto the lawn.

I suppose the apartment was typical. Lots of board games and books, a small pond of dirty shirts, VHS tapes with hand-scrawled labels. And a computer, with a printer! A Macintosh with a case half-brown from cigarette smoke, and gosh, fliers for last night's Abyssal Eyeballs show were still in the printer tray. I had the computer on and was clicking on the folders when he finally came in.

"I had a spare key," he said, triumphantly. "What the hell?" I turned and made a point of staring at his crotch.

"You have complaints?" I said.

"What the hell!" he repeated, his voice still mostly trapped in his throat.

"I knew you were hiding something," I said. "Because I am a fucking genius." I held up the flier. "Didn't know anything about it?"

"I was told you might be coming. Are you someone's sister?"

I snatched a VHS tape at random and waved it around. "Is this child porn?" He sat down, defeated. "What is *Urotsukidoji*?" I said, reading from the label.

"Well, not really child porn. It's an *anime*," he said. "You know, Japanimation?"

"I'm not anyone's sister. Did the older man with the Chelsea girl—"

"Chelsea girl?"

I put a hand to my head and made the shape of bangs with my fingers. "Did he say I was someone's sister? The Chelsea girl's sister."

"He said it was a surprise party for you," the man said. "Uhm . . ."

"What's your name?"

"Joshua. And you're Dawn."

"You have access to the pull lists at the comic store," I said. "It's not hard to guess I was the 'Dawn'—how many other girls are regulars, or buy anything good? I'll perform the Holmesian displays around here."

"How did you know I printed out the fliers?"

"Oh, that I didn't," I admitted. "I just knew you were hiding something, because you made no effort to pretend that you weren't. But now that you mention it, they do kind of look like the fliers the store makes for itself."

"Give me one good reason why I shouldn't call the police right now," Joshua said. "You could have killed me."

"And with both hands, you could have freed yourself, but you were too busy jerking off," I said. "How does it feel, the shoe being on the other foot? You were asking for it, just like a girl in a short skirt."

"Give me one good reason why I shouldn't just kill you and rape you for real," he said then, his voice a cold dead thing. I showed him my Swiss Army knife, and opened the blade.

"That all you got? You can't kill me with that."

"I can ruin your day with it." I showed him my spiked ring too. "And this. And more. And after we had such an intimate moment in your car, too."

Joshua put a hand up to his neck. He'd have a story for work. "Do you always run around striking up conversations and then attacking people?"

"I have been making a habit of it this week," I said. "Listen, the older guy you met, with the girl? He's dead. Shot in the head. I'm trying to figure out who did it, and why."

He laughed. "Maybe he blew his own head off. Ever think of that?"

"That's what the cops think, but I know better."

"Well, I can't help you," he said. "I met the guy once. He bought a shitload of comics—*Watchmen* and *Dark Knight Returns* and all the other stuff we can't keep on the shelves because of all the news and hype. The usual middle-aged guy, except that the girl he was with was actually cute, and not his daughter."

"And how about her? Did you see her again?"

"I did, actually," Joshua said. "She gave me a disk with the little symbol in it." I quickly looked around the table, then realized that he meant the symbol was *in* the disk as a file, not on the disk as a symbol. "She wanted that added to the fliers."

As leads go, it was a thin one, but even if the Chelsea girl wasn't the killer she knew Bernstein and that alone made her worth talking to. Apparently, Bernstein had a type anyway. For a second I imagined her on the other side of the house, peeking in through the other window, seeing Bernstein's body from another angle and coming to the same conclusions I did. And then maybe she attached herself to Greg to get closer to me, almost like I'd forced myself on Joshua.

"Do we look that much alike?" I asked. "Could we really be sisters?" I left myself open, and he took the bait.

"You could be the fat sister," he said, the web of flesh between thumb and forefinger still massaging the streak of red across his neck. "Hell, you could be the guy's daughter. You've got a big nose, like he does. The other girl's older than you. Looks young, but maybe midtwenties, and fucking smoking. She wore this slick silk number that hugged her curves. She looked a little like Dagger from *Cloak and Dagger*—"

"Do you want to be alone with your rape videos and stained pants again?"

"Why don't you get out of here before I change my mind about calling the police."

"I will," I said. I grabbed a crumpled napkin and used it to pluck another videotape, this one unlabeled but clearly used, from a coffee table. "Should I keep this to show them when they come to my house?"

"It's blank," Joshua said blankly.

"Then you won't mind."

"I certainly don't mind at all."

"I'll be on my way then. Do you remember the number for 911?"

"I believe it's 911. You go home and wait for them and show them that blank tape right before they arrest you for attempted murder."

"I'll do that. I'm sure they have a copy of their own in the special jerk-off room right by the coffeemakers and dough-nuts display case."

"That's where I'd set up a jerk-off room for blank tapes, indeed."

"I'll be seeing you then, Joshua."

"You will be."

I sauntered outside. He foolishly didn't open the blinds to watch me leave. I slashed two of his tires so he couldn't follow me, or mow me down, then broke into a mad run. It was a fairly long walk back home, and the sun was dipping low and red. Once again I'd encountered someone who was linked to Bernstein's machinations. I had thought he and I were alone against the world, but I was beginning to realize that we were all somehow connected. A web radiating forth from Bernstein, with only a few strands leading directly to me. But I had names and the beginning of a timeline. I just needed to find my skinny little doppelgänger, the Chelsea girl. Or let her find me.

And then someone else found me. Roderick. He was on a ten-speed and roared past me as I was walking down the synchronistically named Cherub Lane. He waved to me, and I was so shocked that he saw me that I waved back and smiled. My face felt goofy, like a pumpkin with a crooked smile.

He stopped with the soles of his feet right in front of me and smiled back. "Hey," he said. "What brings you out here?"

"Hey, that's an odd thing to ask a single woman, alone and on her own," I said. "Are you a stalker? Are you stalking me?" I took a step forward and licked my lips.

It's important, when encountering young men of fuckable dimensions, to act a little strange at first. It's not quite playing "hard to get," which is just Victorian morality and market-based sexual political economy, but something more. You can take a measure of a man, find out how interesting he is, by challenging him. Would Roderick play the brute to cover up his offense? Would he stammer like a schoolboy? And that's leaving aside the fact that there is no such thing as a coincidence. Whether one believes that we all exist on the currents of aether and spend our lives pushed and nudged about by the Wills of Secret Masters, or if we are just all simply molecules in motion, one thing is true: there are no coincidences.

"I am stalking you," Roderick said. "I was on my way to the Kentucky Fried Chicken, but I am also stalking you. It was a perfect coincidence."

"I see, and why might you be stalking me?"

Roderick blinked. "You mean . . . you don't know? Don't you realize what's going on here? Between us? In the world around us?" Now he was fucking with me. Flirting under conditions of universal alienation from our species-being made it impossible for him to just be honest with me—that's the fate of sex under capitalism. There was something clever on the tip of my tongue, something clever and long enough to reach all the way down to the pit of my stomach, but I stopped. Bernstein was dead. By no means was our relationship a traditional one, not even on the level of mentor and protégé, or mage and Scarlet Woman, but still, he was a dead old loser with a bullet in his head, and only two people in this world cared about that: me, and the person who had killed him. What was I supposed to do? Spread for some kid who either had a condom in his wallet for just such an occasion, or well-rehearsed justification for not ever using one? Fuck that.

"Kid, I'm sorry. I don't know what you're talking about," I told him. "I'm tired." And by saying so, I became tired. "I've got to get home. I'll see you around. It's a small town."

"There's another Abyssal Eyeballs show," Roderick called out after me. "A couple of nights from now! There are things you need to know!"

"I know everything I need to know," I said without turning back, without even glancing over my shoulder. "I am a fucking genius!"

When I got home, Grandma was reading the *TV Guide* slowly, to herself, cheering each jeer and jeering each cheer, and the painting of the Tower was still in front of the television screen.

# 10.

I was up all night. One thing my mother said that always worked for me is this: *When you're anxious or upset at night, go to bed anyway. Even if your mind is racing, your body will get some rest.* There's an interesting little division between mind and body. The Marxists wouldn't have it, but there is something to be gained from seeing oneself as one's own homunculus pulling the levers and turning the cranks of the body. Even if it's not true, it's often best to behave as though it is true. And that's magick. I'd programmed the body well; I was going crazy, getting close to killing someone, finding my limbs doing things that years of school and church and parents should have hardwired them against ever doing. All in the cause of j_____. I was worried that I might soon murder someone. It's not a moral issue, but a practical one. I'd never find Bernstein's killer in prison. The ethics of sacrificing someone . . . Well, there's a long history of bloodletting unto death for ritual or social purposes. "The ethics of the thing appear to have concerned no one; nor, to tell the truth, need they do so," Crowley once wrote. Of course, that particular essay ended with the sentence, "You are also likely to get into trouble over this chapter unless you truly comprehend its meaning."

But I was not truly comprehending anything. What had Bernstein been up to? He knew my father, perhaps even knew me from afar before I met him, owned the home in which I grew up, and even somehow planned the Abyssal Eyeballs show for me. Then there was that Chelsea girl—another me. Maybe even a better me. Was the Hispanic kid also one of Bernstein's? Greg? Bernstein could have planted the painting with him, or simply whipped up another one. Bernstein had seen me coming, after all.

How many points does a unicursal hexagram have? That's a simple question with a simple and inaccurate answer—six. But the line, drawn properly, forms four triangles and a pair of rhomboids and a quartet of quadrilaterals, so there's another twenty-eight, on the inside. The hexagram is all about movement, a dialectic between Abyss and Divinity, and movements always get more complex the more you focus on them. I thought of myself as the center of Bernstein's symbolic life, the five-petaled flower Crowley dropped in the middle of the shape to symbolize heaven, but maybe I was just marooned on some distant tip, and seeing everything from the wrong vantage point.

I couldn't go searching for the Chelsea girl, I decided. Partially because I was annoyed with Greg, and partially because two people on the move would hardly ever find one another. In the morning, I would strike. She would find me. People have a habit of finding me, just as I have a knack for finding them. It's a small town, just like I'd told Roderick.

That morning, I put myself in the center of town. Or rather, right on the border between two villages—Port Jefferson Station and Port Jefferson Village are bisected by the Long Island Rail Road tracks. We have separate zip codes, different post offices, everything. In the dreams of some suburban planner, the Village was for the wealthy and the Station is where the wealthy would keep their maids, and plumbers, and pizza parlors, but the border was a porous one. My father's squat was technically in the Village, and all sorts of rich assholes lived in Port Jefferson Station. I toed the line between the two, literally, by standing on the railroad tracks, right on Main Street. It was just after the morning rush had ended, so there were fewer trains to concern myself with, and more vehicle traffic. The time was right, the conditions were right—I would summon her.

I walked across the tracks to the middle of Main Street and began my reverse breathing—pulling in the belly on the inhales, pushing out the belly on the exhales. A diesel engine idled by the railroad station. I stood between lanes like a traffic cop in an old movie, cars brushing right by me. I could have reached out and adjusted the rearview mirrors as they passed, had I wished to. Time passed quickly. It was so difficult not to think of Chelsea Girl, not to think of a white horse galloping around a church. There was a shudder under my feet, but it was not the big black thing from the Earth's core. Some lever had been thrown on the locomotive engine. I dared not glance at my watch, or that would break the spell. Port Jefferson Station is the terminus of the line, and by definition also the origin, so the trains leaving the station tended to leave on time. But what time was it? Had it been forty-five minutes already?

Here's the thing about using one's Will to go unnoticed. One really has to be nonchalant about it. It's not true invisibility at all—there's no atom-sized black hole conveniently sucking the light in all directions. You're there. You're visible. You just must act *above* notice, and not beneath notice. Humans are predators; we seek out the weak, we crave them. The sniveling coward can never hide. Curling up into a ball practically sends out a cloud of fuck-kill-eat pheromones that attracts sharks in the form of men. But it's hard to be nonchalant when a locomotive is rumbling a few yards away. I finally glanced over. The conductor was still on the platform, his uniform just archaic enough to be comforting. That hat, the blue blazer. From my perspective, on the tracks, waiting to shrug my shoulders and hold a little sit-in of one, I realized for the first time how insanely LIRR personnel dressed. What were the semiotics of those little round caps, the large bills, the metal plate?

The red lights flared and the railroad crossings jerked to life and began to lower. For a moment my Will deserted me and I glanced about nervously. There she was, in a weird white boat of a Volvo, laughing at me, both middle fingers way up. Then she sneered and honked the horn, cranking down her window. "Hey, you stupid bitch!" she shouted. "Get off the tracks!" I bolted, ducked the railroad crossing, and tried her door, but she managed to slam the lock shot with her palm first. The Volvo was an older model, but a big station wagon type; Chelsea Girl had already reached over and locked the passenger side door too before I'd even rounded the corner. I tried the back hatch, but it was also locked. No plates. The train began to pull out of the station. Traffic had backed up, but Chelsea Girl threw the car in reverse and tried to edge me out. I grabbed the roof rack and pulled myself up onto the car's ridiculously huge rubber bumper. She stopped just before backing her rear, and my own, into the car immediately behind us. Now everyone started yelling, hooting, honking their car horns. The train roared past and I howled, joyously. At least something was leaving Long Island for fabled Mannahatta. *Lo! Upsprang the aboriginal name!*

Chelsea Girl wasn't going to speed off; traffic was always a crawl down Main Street, and a cop car was generally idling nearby in case someone decided to cause some trouble for the railroad. Main Street also had a semisecret identity as Route 25A, a state road. And state roads meant state troopers. A very visible me hanging from the rear of her car—one sans license plates—limited her choices even more severely than they limited mine. When the rail crossings rose, she drove immediately into the train station parking lot. I ran around to the passenger side, hoping she didn't store a revolver in the glove compartment. The air didn't smell like death just then, but I hadn't quite determined whether Chelsea Girl was an intelligent person or just some arbitrary bitch as of yet. She reached over and unlocked the door. I got in, locked it again, planted a boot against the glove box, and told her to get a move on, but she was smart enough to do that. The parking lot had another exit, so we took that one and drove out onto Railroad Avenue, which was sooty and underdeveloped, like a patch of acne on a cute face. Like Chelsea Girl's face, I noticed now. She was younger than I had imagined. Maybe a sophomore, with makeup troweled on like a high hair on her way to the mall. It was the haircut that was out of place; that was her invisibility.

"Where are we going?" I asked.

"You know where," the Chelsea girl said.

"What's your name?"

She glanced up at her reflection in the rearview mirror. "Chelsea will do."

So Bernstein had had another girl. Was I his girl? Maybe Chelsea actually went all the way with him. But I'd never seen her around before, and there are few enough punks around the North Shore that we mostly all know one another. But her haircut was new. Maybe Bernstein had put her up to it—a bit of antinomian praxis. I grinned to myself, imagining some high hair chucking her Aqua Net into the Long Island Sound, then getting on her knees before Bernstein to submit to a head shaving.

"So Chelsea, how did Bernstein get you to fuck him?" I asked. "What did he show you?"

"Maybe I'm the one who showed him a thing or two," she said. The Volvo had a very loud blinker. "Maybe I was the teacher, and he was the student."

"I doubt that."

"Because I'm young. Because I'm a woman. Because you're ineffectual, and so you think all young women must be ineffectual. Looking for *daddy*, princess?" She pulled up close to what was left of Bernstein's house but then drove past it and off the road. The Volvo steered onto a secret path, one little more than a pair of tire ruts, and climbed a grade up behind the house and into a clearing. There were plenty of branches, snapped and hanging from trees, and littering the floor of the clearing, but Chelsea wasn't worried about scratching her car.

I realized that I was making assumptions. When I looked at Chelsea, I'd been seeing myself—a doppelgänger. I just assumed she had been with Bernstein, had been enamored of him, like I was. She was being cagey, trying to get something out of me just as I was with her . . . because she didn't know very much about Bernstein after all. The "Jewish-looking" guy Joshua said she had been with at the comic shop could have been anybody. Hell, it could have been my father. Even in his saner days, he'd come home from work on Friday nights, upset, when a Lubavitcher would stop him on the street and ask if he were Jewish. "My father's big fucking nose," he'd say.

"I'm looking, but you found yourself a daddy, didn't you?" I said. "Nice Volvo, by the way. Did you have to promise to load and unload the dishwasher every night for a week to get to borrow it?"

"I have a job," she said. "Get out of the car." I hustled out before she did and led the way down to the ridge right over Bernstein's plot of land. Another epiphany: this would be a great vantage point for someone interested in Bernstein's way of life, and my own comings and goings. Chelsea had been watching me watch Bernstein. I told her as much.

"You're a fucking genius, aren't you?" she said.

"And you didn't kill him."

"Of course not."

"You wouldn't bring me here if you had," I said.

"No, I wouldn't. Unless I was some psychopath," she said.

"Of course, some might argue that magick is a course in applied psychosis."

The local weather turned cold in a moment. Chelsea's face was flushed, as if she had sucked all the molecular motion in the air into her pores.

"Is that what he told you? Was it all a joke to you?" There was a razor in her throat now. No more Long Island tough girl; she really meant it.

"Yes. No," I said. Then I added, "Maybe." My grandmother used to do that—cover every possible answer—before her memory left her. "But regardless of what he told me, you know it's true." I didn't even know whether or not she was talking about Bernstein at all, who had never called magick *applied psychosis* in so many words. But it was true. It is true.

Chelsea narrowed her eyes. "So, is that why you did it?"

"I didn't kill Bernstein, if that's what you're asking." I was amazed at how casual the words sounded coming out of my mouth. Chelsea was too.

"That's not what I was asking!" she said. "You know what you did!"

"I don't know a goddamn thing, except that I know nothing."

"We're both just trying to baffle one another with bullshit," she said after a long moment. She glanced down at the cabin, and pointed her chin at it. "I've seen you skulking around here. And in Port Jeff too. You're so fucking ridiculous. You're like a cartoon villain hiding behind a bush and lifting it up to sneak around, tiny feet going *dinka-dinka-dinka*."

"Nice haircut," I told her. "Is it new?"

"I was here that night when you looked through the window, and then stumbled backward, then started running."

"I wouldn't call it running . . ."

Chelsea gave me the once-over. "Yeah, I wouldn't call it running either." A middle-class bitch with a middle-class joke, despite her new lifestyle. No surprises, except what came next.

"He killed himself, you know. Bernstein was all about changing his life to test himself, to find his true Will underneath all the rubbish of society."

"But—"

"He shot himself with his off hand," Chelsea said. "Think about it: the guy on the left-handed path, who happens to be left handed. Who is committed to living life to its fullest finding death with his right hand."

I shook my head. "Poetic, but bullshit." Chelsea had nothing to say to that. I told her, "Just because you didn't see anyone come in or out of the house doesn't mean Bernstein killed himself. I presume you got a police report and read about the gun. You're just trying to get me to say something, or do something. There's something you want."

"Oh, I already have what I want. I just want to keep it," Chelsea said, but not to me. She glanced away, beyond Bernstein's house.

"Did you bring me here to get a confession out of me? Just to let me know that you've been watching me?"

"Hey girl, you're the one who's been looking for me. You jumped on the back of my fucking car."

"What was your relationship to Bernstein?"

Chelsea twisted her lips, thinking. Then she said, "He was
. . . a friend of a friend. I wasn't sucking his dick or anything,
not like some nameless sluts that come to mind."

I filed that away—both the information and the attack. I
had nothing else to say to her, but I knew I'd see Chelsea
again. If she were my doppelgänger it stood to reason, for
some definition of reason, that she might have her own
version of Bernstein. Perhaps the right-handed suicide she
knew was my left-handed murder victim, or perhaps there
was another person much like Bernstein out there somewhere
on the North Shore of Long Island. A rival.

"You can tell me about whose dick you are sucking any
time you like, Chelsea," I said, smiling. "We can trade Manic
Panic colors and share tips on avoiding infections in our
nipple piercings, just like a couple of punk rock girls at a
slumber party, 'kay?"

Chelsea smiled back. "Dyke," she said. Then she walked
over to her car, got in, and started the engine. I knew I wasn't
going to get a lift back.

# 11.

At the best of times, the walk home from Bernstein's is a long one, one suited for sultry August nights when the fireflies outnumber the mosquitoes. It had only been a couple of months before when I'd walk home and imagine sweating out the black poisons of the day. And I'd be safe, unseen by road traffic or anyone else except maybe that old devil moon in the otherwise empty sky. But Chelsea had seen me, or so she said. Did she see me that night when Bernstein did his trick; did she see the satyr crash through the window and run into the woods?

This afternoon was colder than chilly. An autumnal near frost, the wind fueled by the Long Island Sound. It hurt my bones, the wind did, and I decided to walk into it. When I was a kid my father took me to the docks at the edge of Port Jefferson and explained to me that my second grade teacher was wrong—Christopher Columbus didn't discover that the world was round. The ancients knew it, from peering out at the horizon and watching ships come in over the curve of the Earth. And we waited for a ship to come in, but the sandbars and the fact that the Sound was only about twenty miles wide ruined our chance.

I walked up into Belle Terre to check on the Riley family of cardboard-pizza eaters. I was curious whether they'd be home—were they Wall Street types who commuted three hours each way to enjoy their stainless steel freezer full of frozen foods, or were they Old Money who just happened to "have" their riches in the same way the rest of us have a pair of ears? It was midafternoon by the time I got to their house, and the low sun painted the stonework in yellows, oranges, and reds. I expected that either the house would be dark and empty, except perhaps for an overweight Latina with a push broom, or that the couple would be home, enjoying doughnuts and cider in their J. Crew sweaters. Reality without Will often conforms to cliché, after all.

The cleaning lady wasn't Latina, but she was otherwise what one might expect from Belle Terre—it was the old Greek lady who had the fifteen cats at her own house about a mile away, with her usual shuffling gait and an old black dress and cardigan. She was in the kitchen, mostly keeping herself busy. Her car wasn't in the driveway; perhaps Belle Terre had local rules to keep aged automobiles out of the development, and she had had to walk up the long and winding path to get here.

And the man was home in the enormous living room. Disappointingly, he wasn't in drag, or nude and swinging from a noose, or fucking a ten-year-old boy. He was watching television. CNN. Protesters in the GDR again. What a huge television it was, practically the size of one of the walls of my bedroom at Grandma's apartment. He had something in his lap: a white bread sandwich. And he lifted half of it—did the maid cut it diagonally for him on request or out of long-standing habit?—to his rich face and bit into it like an animal, his cheeks stuffed. Did watching history end before his very eyes give him an erection? The inevitable triumph of capitalism must have made his Wonder Bread taste extra special, I'm sure.

Suddenly, I was sick. My stomach turned inside out and started crawling up my throat. This was something other than Will; it was pure autonomic response. My arms moved, herky-jerky, and picked up one of the bleached white rocks at my feet.

The shrubbery was lined with them. I threw it at a window and it bounced off. Then I screamed, picked it and a few more up, and flung them at the window with both hands. A clatter, then a scatter. Not even a scratch. High-tech, high-security stuff designed to look just like every other early twentieth-century mansion in Belle Terre. He didn't even hear it.

I avoided the comic shop and the rest of downtown Port Jefferson, though I hadn't eaten and was getting very hungry. I even stayed off Main Street, in case someone recognized me from my morning antics at the LIRR. I thought to try to find Roderick, but given how my last stunt with finding someone had gone, I thought the better of it. Greg, I could talk to, if only to warn him away from Chelsea.

How strange my libido was. It was an animal of its own, a lioness in the cage of my skull. I was in mourning for an older man, on a mission of j_____. No, a mission of revenge. I had spent the last couple of years purposefully alienating myself from the local boys, with Twinkies and Manic Panic and a cultivated surliness. And now I was jealous of another girl, and desirous of cock my own age. Hell, had Riley turned around after I'd thrown that rock I probably would have offered to suck his dick too. Learn a little capitalist magick for once, maybe.

I was surprised to find Greg and Roderick together, in Greg's front yard. Greg was raking the leaves, or panto-miming the same, working over the same mud-brown pile. Roderick stood on the curb, smoking a cigarette. I saw them before they saw me and got a chance to listen in for a few seconds.

"—all fucked up," Greg said.

"The whole world is, it's true," Roderick said. "Ever see that movie, *Something Wicked This Way Comes*? It's like that—a storm is coming."

"The seller of lightning rods arrived before the storm," I said as I walked up to them.

"I didn't even read it. I think I saw the movie once," Greg said. "Oh, hi, Dawn."

"You guys know each other?"

"Who do you think the lightning rod seller is?" Roderick asked me.

"Maybe a better question is who the lightning rod is, Rod."

"I've known Roderick for a long time. Forever even." Greg leaned on the rake as if his labors of several minutes had exhausted him. "We took tae kwon do together when we were seven."

"I went to Catholic school. My mother used to drive me all the way out to Huntington and back every day," Roderick said.

"Is that what you two were doing? Reminiscing about karate class?"

"*Tae kwon do*," Greg said.

"We were talking about all the weird shit going on lately," Roderick said.

"You told him about Bernstein," I said to Greg, who just shrugged. "What other weird shit is going on lately?" I asked Roderick.

It was his turn to shrug, but he answered, "Well, there was the Abyssal Eyeballs."

"Which you were a part of."

"Like I said, I just had a feeling," Roderick said.

"Is that what they taught you in Catholic school—to get in touch with your feelings?" I wanted to smile at him, at both of them, really. But I couldn't.

"I've been doing house shows for a while—"

"Out in Huntington?" Greg said.

"Yeah. Catholic-school girls like anything transgressive," Roderick said. He shot me a look out of the corner of his eye.

"Ha, I noticed," Greg said.

"Is this how guys talk when there are no girls around, boys?" That shut them up. "Good boys. You should stop smoking, Rod. And Greg, don't you own any non—Iron Maiden T-shirts? There's no reason to play Casanova Badass with me."

"What do you want?" Greg said, petulant.

"Remember that girl at the show? The one whose esophagus you cleaned out with your tongue? She's a bad penny, that one. If there's weird shit going down, I guarantee you that she's involved in it."

"And you're not?" Greg said.

"Yeah, maybe you're the lighting rod seller," Rod said.

"I'm the lightning rod," I told them. "And I'm not a commodity, not a capital good. I am the thing in itself, a use value."

"Okay, I'm confused," Greg said.

"Good," I said, and I turned on my heel and walked off, waiting just a moment too long before appending *bye* to the word *good*. Roderick launched into an explanation of Marxism for Greg as I turned the corner. He must have been educated by Jesuits.

It was twilight by the time I picked my way through the side streets and back to the apartment, and when I walked in the police were there in the kitchen, waiting for me, and Grandma was sitting at the table, sobbing like a toddler.

"Look at you," one of the cops said. There were five of them—there had never been so many people in the apartment, not even when Grandma had fallen last year and the EMTs had come—and they all were smirking. "Halloween isn't for another three weeks, fuckin' freak."

"Murder . . ." Grandma whispered.

# 12.

I'm not a huge fan of the show *I Love Lucy*, but of course I've seen every episode. Despite my interests in magick, over-throwing capitalism, and punk rock, I'm still living in the suburbs of the United States, and my grandmother owns a television. Of course I watched it as a kid, and like most people I have a favorite scene. A kabbalist might call my reminiscence about Lucy an example of Qliphoth—an impure "husk" left behind after the moment of Divine Emanation.

Anyway, my favorite scene isn't the one on the chocolate factory assembly line—though is there a better example of speed-up and increased exploitation in popular culture?—or Lucy's drunken attempt to sell Vitameatavegamin, a classic critique of consumerism and bourgeois medical "science." My favorite scene is from the episode when Tennessee Ernie Ford plays Lucy's hick "Cousin Ernie" from Tennessee. He got lost on the way to the Ricardos' fancy Manhattan apart-ment, and walked across Long Island to find it.

"You walked all the way from Long Island?" Lucy asks, incredulous.

"Yup. Ding-donged if it ain't," Ernie answers.

"What?"

"A loooooong island," Ernie says.

When I was a kid, family legend had it that I would only eat when *I Love Lucy* was on TV. Luckily for my mother, and for me, Channel 5 aired it three times a day, and around breakfast time, lunch, and dinner. I don't even remember the first time

I saw my favorite scene, but of course I remember the first time I remember—I was six, and it was five o'clock, and the Long Island scene came on and I squealed with excitement. "Lucy knows about Long Island! She made a joke about Long Island!"

"You say that every time," my mother had said, but I hadn't remembered anything that had ever been so thrilling. The pretty woman who called herself a redhead even though she was clearly in black and white had somehow acknowledged my existence, just as I worshiped her thrice daily. *I've been looking for that moment again ever since.* Bernstein told me that one could dig enlightenment from Qliphoth, and there we go—I just did.

I had thought of my favorite scene from *I Love Lucy* for a fairly banal reason: Long Island is very long. The pigs arrested me for Bernstein's murder, cuffed me, took me downstairs and around the back where their three black-and-whites were hiding, near the apartment complex's garbage bin. They shoved me in the back seat of one of the cars, hit their sirens and lights, and we sped down to Riverhead. It was a long trip. This is a loooong island. The sun was down when we got to the county lockup.

My look did not go over well in the holding cell. There were three other women, all black, older than me, and members of the lumpenproletariat, in holding. We all wore our civilian clothes—the presumption of innocence, you see, despite the bars and the desk pig's rape threats, though they did take away my boots—and they wore cheap T-shirts despite the autumnal chill. One was still in sandals. There were about as many teeth in my head as there were in between them. I had a racist thought when they turned to look at me as one, when their chatter ceased—*Do these girls know each other? Are they a gang? Are they gonna jump me?* No, they were strangers to one another.

"Who the fuck are you?" said one woman, who looked like a collection of five broomsticks. "A punk rocker?"

One of the others, who, I realized as she spoke, was actually sitting on the cell's toilet and taking a shit, said, "That's pretty obvious."

The third just stared. I wanted to stare back. I could have won any staring contest, easily, but there were three of them to keep track of. *Of them.* That old racist flinch. Isn't every man and woman a star? "I won't be here for long," I said. "You can get on with your evening in a bit."

"What you don here for?" the toilet woman asked.

I wasn't sure if *don* was "done" or "down" but I told her half a lie. "They say I killed my boyfriend, but it wasn't me." The girl who was staring at me kept staring, but now she was smiling.

"It wasn't none of us," said the toilet woman.

"Who was it?" said the first woman, then she laughed. "Who killed your man?" They all laughed at that, then started speaking amongst themselves, about me, as though I wasn't there. I was the dumb white bitch who certainly didn't have a boyfriend because I looked like the devil, and I probably was a chickenhead, and I was an ugly cunt as well. The staring woman had joined in on the conversation too, but without taking her eyes from me.

Obviously, Chelsea was the lightning rod seller, and she had sold me out to the pigs. Maybe the trip out to Bernstein's was just to give the cops time to show up at the apartment and terrify my grandmother. My grandmother, who could already have tried to make herself dinner, like she used to, but one lapse in her attention and the kitchen would go up in flames. It was extremely important that I not care about this at all, to match my doppelgänger emotion for emotion, thought for thought. And then, find a way to take one step beyond where she was, to get the better of her.

I had the feeling that the cops didn't take the murder charge all that seriously. Nobody did. There had been no news van outside, no more than the usual sneers any punk on Long Island gets from the pigs, no interrogation or even casually incriminating conversation on the long drive over. The pigs who had arrested me didn't even glance at me in the rearview mirror. There was a force at work beyond the state, that dark thing that lived under the sands of the island, that lived out in the Sound. It had no more of an interest in j_____ than I did, but it was moving with a Will of its own to run interference for me, I could feel it.

The starer decided that she wanted my shirt, which was a man's Hanes pocket T-shirt I'd decorated with a Sharpie. Admittedly, it was still in better shape than hers. "Take it off," she told me. The air in the cell changed.

"Fuck off," I said. "Dyke." I added that last bit to make her angry, but she just kept simmering.

"I don't care about your titties, white girl. I just want that shirt."

She didn't want the shirt. She wanted to humiliate me, and to bond with the others in the cell. The others who belonged here, and knew it, and resented me for not belonging. And they were right; something was very wrong with my presence here, and I wouldn't be staying long. But there was no way I was going to lose this little game either, and no way I was going to let her beat me up, so I played the card I was dealt.

"In that case," I said, "here you go." And I reached down and pulled the shirt over my head, folded it sloppily, and handed it to her. My bra was black and leopard print, and got an appreciative snicker from the woman on the toilet, who I then realized had stopped shitting. She was playing a game of her own. Would we have to beg for our chance to use the commode, and thank her for warming it for us, later?

"That's right, here I go, you fucking fat white bitch," the starer said. I stared back at her this time. The locus of power had shifted sufficiently. *This must be what Scarlet Women feel like*, I found myself thinking. *Omnipotent, not vulnerable, in their nakedness.*

"Your stomach," the starer said, blinking. My stomach had a little bit of a gut, and it was crisscrossed with gashes from those moments when I slipped and dared think about j_____. "Your man do that to you?"

I looked down, frowned, then shrugged. "No, it was me."

"Why do you do that for?"

"To remind myself that nobody ever gets, or deserves, an even break," I said.

The first woman laughed. "I could have told you that already, child." And with that the mood lifted. It was chilly in the cell, and the women made no room for me either on the benches or on the floor near the vent, so I stood all night, hands in front of my belly in a *zhan zhuang* pose, just breathing in and out, trying to empty my mind and fill it with my body.

Breakfast was McDonald's—Egg McMuffin, no hash browns, no coffee because coffee could be a weapon. The three women drank water, I took nothing, but the smell of industrial grease agitated my stomach and drove me wild. My mouth was full of saliva when I was finally led to the phone to make my phone call. A guard gave me an orange top, which was flimsier than a hospital gown, to wear for my walk down the hall. Someone had written PRESUMED INNOCENT on the back with a smelly Magic Marker so that I would not be confused with actual convicted criminals. That was one of the few rituals of legality, for the law is a magick all its own that exists as pure Logos with hardly any intersection with the world of material creation, given to me. Still no

interrogation, no hint of a public defender, not even a mention
of a murder charge. At the phone, which was an old pay phone
rigged with steel bars for some reason, I realized that I had
nobody to call. I wracked my brains for a moment, then asked
for the White Pages. My first instinct was to open to a random
page and stab at it with my finger, then call that person, but
then I realized that Greg was in the book. Not that he had any
money. But he did answer the phone. It was a Saturday
morning.

"Greg, it's Dawn. I'm in Riverhead, at the jail."

"Holy shit."

"Listen, I need you to do something for me . . ." I said. Then
I explained that I wanted him to go over to Stony Brook—
"Take the bus; it's only a dollar and it arrives at Meat Farms
every hour on the hour, Jesus Christ!" I had to tell him—and
to find some Red Submarine flier or leaflet or pamphlet. The
campus was littered with them. Then call that number, and
ask for Mike, and arrange for him to come down to the jail,
maybe with an attorney, to find out what was going on with
charges or bond or an arraignment on my behalf.

"Uh, why would he even do any of that?" Greg asked.

"Because he's a Marxist. And he has money."

"How do you know he has money?"

"Because he's a Marxist! Poor people on Long Island don't
care about Marxism. It's a rich person's hobby, like collecting
vintage decoy ducks." The guard stiffened. "I have to go, just
do it! Blowjobs for everyone, after the revolution!"

I had no idea if Greg would go to Stony Brook, or manage
to find Mike's number, or if he could even be bothered to call
Mike. I would have asked Roderick, but I didn't have his
number, and he was a bit too independently minded. Maybe
I should have just sent Greg to find out what happened to
Grandma. Did the state get its paws on her? Maybe that would

be for the best. Worse—they could have somehow got in contact with Dad, who might even now be in the apartment, shoving jewels and tchotchkes into a pillowcase, or maybe even liberating the television. Or perhaps he was done with his new exotic lifestyle of squatting in abandoned buildings with crack whores, and decided to just move himself in and "take care" of Grandma.

Very convenient for him, my incarceration.

The holding cell remained empty for most of the afternoon. Lunch was a bologna sandwich. That is, a thin, and small, circle of bologna between two pieces of Wonder Bread. I had to open the sandwich to see what I was eating. When I took a bite, I realized that this must have been what the man in Belle Terre was eating yesterday. Pretty much any other cold cut would have been visibly obvious to me from my vantage point.

Afternoon turned to evening, and no Mike. Two more women entered the holding cell—one was an older white woman who had been thoroughly beaten. Her eyes were swollen shut and she had to feel around to find the bench. Soon enough they took her away, presumably for either medical treatment or another beating of some sort. Then the toilet woman was returned to the cell.

"Hookin'," she said, as though it explained everything, which it almost did. But she was led away after only about an hour of silence, and McDonald's burgers for each of us for dinner. "Yesterday was assault," she explained between bites.

It was after 9 p.m. when Mike Schmidt strolled into view, guards on either side of him. He had a big pumpkin face and his eyes were broad. "Wow," he said, "wow. Guess what— you're gonna get to go home, real soon. How did you know I was an attorney?"

"I'm a genius," I told him. "I bet a lot of people tell you that you don't come off as the law school type, eh?"

"Exactly—especially my law professors," Mike said. "So I dropped out after a year and read for the law. You can still do that in New York. Anyway, I want to be alone with my client," he told the guards, who released me from the cell, then put us in a dumpy little room.

"They're listening in," we told one another, and then Mike reached over the table at which we were sitting and punched me lightly in the arm. "Jinx, owe me your soul," he said. "Or a Coke, since there is no such thing as a soul.

"It doesn't matter that they're listening in. They totally fucked up. You're not up on murder charges. You're a person of interest. The problem is your grandmother." He did that tedious quote gesture with his fingers. "'They didn't know' that she had dementia. When they came by to question you— to harass you, really, in the hope that they might find some drugs or that they could bring you in on some kind of disorderly conduct charge if you got uppity—she apparently confessed on your behalf. Anyway, the plus side is that some girl who kind of looks like you also called in to say that she had some information and that she had seen you around the scene of the crime—"

In that moment, the marrow in my spine turned to fire. It shot out the top of my head, melting the ceiling, rising into the sky as a great and flaming fist, red and yellow fingers licking the dark clouds, boiling the moisture in the air; it reached across towns like a solar flare touching the Earth, found Chelsea wherever she was, and destroyed her utterly. I shifted in my chair anyway, and kept from blurting out anything that the pigs could later use against me. But Chelsea was a dead woman.

"Anyway, there's enough confusion and enough embarrassment that they're ready to release you, into my custody. You won't be charged."

I raised my eyebrow. Mike understood. "Well, you're still a 'person of interest,' remember? So they don't just want you going home. You might try to leave town. You might do something to your grandmother—that's their story anyway—to shut her up in case her claims were the result of a lucid moment instead of the usual dementia. So, uh—"

"You sure say 'anyway' frequently," I said.

"Anyway," he said. Then he laughed at himself. "By any Way necessary," and yes, I heard the capital *W* in the way Mike said *Way*. "Though there is only one way."

"The way that ends with me coming home with you."

"You can stay here if you like," Mike said. I didn't like. "'Here' meaning both in the care of the Suffolk County Department of Corrections, and in the prison of individuality and individualism," he added.

"Let's go," I said.

Bernstein always prided himself on being what Eugene V. Debs had called a contradiction in terms: an unorganized socialist. He'd done his time selling papers on the street corners and attending protests; he had even headed down to West Virginia to work among the coal miners. For the experience. What he'd found is a bunch of college kids from Brown, with trust funds, playing Che Guevara and Leon Trotsky, so he had retreated into his books. *Like Lenin, who in the wake of the collapse of the 1905 revolution, retreated into Hegel in order to better understand the dynamics of history*, Bernstein had told me. Mike Schmidt, on the other hand, had no such pride. He just couldn't help himself. He had to be the center of the revolution, and every act was revolutionary. Bailing me out was a fatal blow against police repression, his broad hints about me staying with him for a while was an attempt to smash bourgeois notions of romantic love and commodified sexual relations both. When he ran a red light, that was the revolution. When he stopped for the next one, that was also the revolution. When we made it back to the apartment, Mike parked in a tow-away zone and insisted on coming upstairs. "I want to meet your grandmother, perhaps help calm her. She's probably highly agitated. All those strangers yelling at her."

"And you won't yell at her, not like those other strangers," I said.

"Not unless she requires it."

Mike was a lot like Bernstein, but stupid and needy. And Grandma was gone. The place was messed up. "Tossed," Mike said, though I was sure that all the cops had left with me when I was arrested, and not *everything* was tossed. My room was in its usual semichaotic state, but the drawers hadn't been overturned, and my overnight bag was in the closet, packed. I grabbed it and went through the rest of the apartment. Some silver candlesticks were gone, as were a bunch of Grandma's clothes, and a few pictures. Some of the forks, and the KFC bucket in the fridge, had also vanished. So had the painting of the Tower.

"You can't call the police," Mike said. "You can't call 911. They'll just arrest you again. You're a person of interest, and this can be seen as probable cause. Lots of criminals have the bright idea to whack a family member, then call 911."

"Whack," I said. "You watch a lot of television for a revolutionary Communist."

"The ruling class presents its ideology in a very straightforward way; I'd be stupid not to watch several hours of television every day. But what I am saying is true."

"I don't call 911. I think Grandma either ran off by herself, or my father caught wind of all this and came to get her, and some stuff to sell for crack money," I said. Mike looked at me, surprised. "My father loves crack," I explained. "He was squatting downtown. We can—" I stopped. I couldn't exactly consort with a known drug user either, and Mike had turned pale.

"If he's in some kind of crack frenzy"—Mike *did* watch too much television—"he might come back, thinking that there were some valuables left to steal. You should come home with me tonight." Now I knew where the blood that had been in his face and limbs had gone. Disgusting, but were my sentiments regarding my grandmother any different? I loved an illusion. Materially, the contents of the bag of chemical reactions that made all that I had loved as a child was degrading, like batteries left so long in a Walkman that they leak, corrode, and ruin everything. Grandma was a weakness for me, but the painting was still a clue. My father had them both, probably.

"All right, I will," I said. I wondered if he'd like my leopard-print bra, or my scars. Would he dare to touch them?

Mike's apartment was close to Stony Brook—a few more minutes across Looooong Island—and looked like typical shared graduate student digs, but Mike lived alone. The bookshelves were all cinder blocks and 4 x 4s, and they were jammed with Marxist texts, religious nonsense in English and a few Asian languages, science fiction paperbacks, and the Beats and existentialists. The furniture was scarred and sagging; there were three couches in the living room, and through the open door to Mike's room I saw the bed topped with two mounds of dirty jeans—one for black, and one for blue—and the whole place smelled like patchouli and burned rice. A cat, no, three cats, scattered when we entered, though Mike *tssk-tssk-tssked* for them. The television was on, running TV-55, our thrilling local channel. Mike muttered *Jaws II* to himself, but thankfully didn't expect me to sit down and watch it with him. He turned the set off as he passed by it.

I pushed a box of leaflets and Red Submarine zines off the cushion of one of the couches, grabbed the nearest book—which was, and there are no coincidences, Hegel's *Phenomenology of Spirit*—and read while Mike putzed around, pretending to arrange his apartment for some purpose other than him fucking me, when all he really wanted to do is fuck me. Or fuck anyone, I suppose. I read aloud as he rushed back from the bedroom with a plastic laundry hamper full of foul clothing, and then to the kitchen to put on some tea and to find a bottle of wine that hadn't gone bad in the fridge. "The concrete content, which sensuous certainty furnishes, makes this *prima facie* appear to be the richest kind of knowledge, to be even a knowledge of endless wealth—a wealth to which we can as little find any limit when we traverse its extent in space and time, where that content is presented before us, as when we take a fragment out of the abundance it offers us and by dividing and dividing seek to penetrate its intent." Mike halted, for a moment, both in the way in to the room when I hit the word *sensuous* and on the way back, with the wine, when I hit the word *penetrate*.

"We can fuck if you want," I told him. "I don't come, though. I don't care if you do. It'll be pretty awful, as the first time with someone new generally is, especially when they don't like each other so much—"

"I like you, Dawn—" he started.

"It's not mutual. I appreciate that you sprung me, and gave me a ride back, but it sounded like I was going to be let out sooner rather than later anyway. I don't owe you a fuck, but fucking isn't any worse, or better, than shaking someone's hand. I know you seem very excited about it, and I am willing since it seems to be an acceptable way to end the evening, and I'll have to ask you another favor soon enough, but it isn't going to be fun," I said. "What I mean to say is, don't worry about your dirty sheets, or the sock smell, or whether you'll fumble with the condom for a minute and then go soft and have to jerk yourself off to get hard again. I won't reach down to put you in me, Mr. Red Submarine; you'll have to squirm around to find the slot yourself like an idiot. So don't drink too much."

"Well, I find it easier with doggy style anyway," Mike said. He drank from the bottle, smiled, and handed it to me. Not a bad comeback, all things considered. "So, have you read much Hegel?"

"Just those sentences. I can see why you like them." I took a drink. "It's gibberish. Stuff is all over the place. Look at it, but don't *take a look at it*. Not to start anyway. Gotcha."

"So you think it's nonsense, but you're a Marxist yourself," he said, and he sat down next to me. We were going to fuck after all. Oh, well.

"Nonsense, but nonsense in the way that's close to the truth," I said. Then I dropped my voice an octave and said, "We are to conquer the Illusion, to drive it out. The slaves that perish are better dead."

"Did I sense a capital *I* in the word *illusion*," Mike asked, "or was that itself an illusion? Where's the quote from? Nietzsche?"

"Crowley," I said.

"Oh, brother," he said. Then he leaned in and started kissing my neck. "Talk about the prison of individuality," he said. His hand was on my belly. I was still wearing my orange county-issue top. The scars across my stomach would not stop Mike. "I've already shattered the Illusion, Dawn," he said. "That's how I was able to act so quickly, to take a call from a stranger to go help another stranger. We're all connected."

"We're going to be anyway," I said. Now he had a titful with one hand and with the other he snaked between my back and the couch to turn me to him for a kiss. I gave him one, closed lipped. "I need to find my grandmother tomorrow. And something else too. Do you know how to look up deeds? I want to know who owns the house my grandmother used to own."

"We will, I do. According to my ability and according to your needs," he said. "Do you want to go into the bedroom?" I said sure, and we did, and he was rather expert with the condom after all and his bed squeaked like an old shoe. On my hands and knees, he couldn't see much of my front, which was fine with me.

At 3 a.m. he woke me up and asked what I thought of the situation in the Eastern bloc. Before I could answer, he told me that it was very exciting, that he saw the possibility of the deformed workers' states solving their own bureaucratic excesses via working-class self-activity, and thus leading to a true socialist second world that we could both inhabit. He literally used the word "inhabit." I told him that he was fucking dreaming, but he thought I meant to say that he was talking in his sleep.

# 13.

Mike Schmidt knew a lot of social workers, and true to his word he started making calls at two minutes after nine. He didn't make breakfast, or even offer to go out and get Dunkin' Donuts. I drank water from the tap—I had to wash a glass myself, and even the sink was dirty—and waited at the kitchen table, flipping through some RS pamphlets, which were mostly about campus issues and reminiscences of the 1960s, when he was an undergrad. The phone was in the living room. Red Submarine, so far as I could tell, seemed to be composed of Schmidt, whoever he was fucking at the time, a random and ever-changing assortment of sophomores who are purged when they declare an unacceptable major, and a few perennial graduate students. And Bernstein. *Comrade J* anyway, according to the caption under the photo in the zine I was reading. There was no real discussion of what Comrade J was doing, or even why his picture was in the pamphlet. Bernstein was filler. His sideburns were so thick they looked like a pair of bushy wings. I guessed 1974 or so. Even the sign he was holding appeared to be blank, though much of it was cropped out of the frame.

"Hey," I called out, "Do you have a job? I mean, do I need to leave soon?"

Mike swung his head into the doorway. "I don't. Back in 1979 Public Safety beat me during a demo and broke my leg in three places. I sued SUNY and got a huge settlement. It's what inspired me to read the law too." Then the phone rang, and he ducked back into the living room. After some murmuring he returned and said, "Well, the good news is that your grandmother wasn't taken in anywhere. Nor has she been found by the cops, and she's not in any public hospitals anywhere in Suffolk County. So she's not in the clutches of the state. And no, you can't leave. You've been released into my custody, remember?"

I just stared at him. Grandma wasn't home when we had swung by the apartment the previous night. She had no friends, nobody to turn to, and no kindly stranger was going to be able to put up with her for long. "So, she's not in the clutches of the state. But I am, and you are. After all, if I leave that means you have to follow me. Aren't we both trapped, after a fashion?"

"Oh, you can leave. I was just teasing. Anyway, I just have to make sure you don't leave the county, basically, and if the cops want to talk to you, that you'll be available . . ." Mike trailed off. He was trapped, he realized finally.

"Let's go find my grandmother," I said. She had to be with my father, unless he just took the stuff and left the door open behind him, for her to wander through, lost and confused and cold in her house dress and slippers.

"Thanks for last night," he said in the car. He listened to WBAB. Led Zeppelin and Pink Floyd and such. I told him that I couldn't believe he listened to this shit, and he launched into a monologue about rock and the 1960s and the nature of power in culture and I didn't have to talk about our sex thanks to his narcissism, so I was quite pleased with myself.

Then I asked about Bernstein. "Comrade J, eh?" Mike said. "Yeah, he was a character, but aren't we all?"

"You often confuse being abstruse with being enigmatic, and being enigmatic with being intelligent, you know?" I asked.

"Hey, I like that. Mind if I borrow it? We'll have to write it down later." Mike wasn't being sarcastic.

"Anyway," I said.

"Yeah, Jay. Nice guy, I guess. Into some heavy stuff. A real ultraleft. Any nationalistic dictator who waved a red flag, he'd support. A genius, a very clever guy. He read maybe eight or nine languages. If not for his politics, he could have worked for the United Nations pretty easily, but he spent a lot of his time corresponding with radicals all over the world. I was never quite sure what he was getting at, though. He expected the revolution to happen without putting in the hard work a revolutionary needs to put in."

"What work would that be?" I asked.

"I stopped trying to figure that out long ago. That's why I'm a Marxist of the Tao," he said. And we were there.

The squat seemed unoccupied. When I kicked open the door, Mike said, "Wow." He added, looking around, "What a mess."

"Really? It's less cluttered than your digs," I said. And it was less cluttered than it had been. A lot of dust and broken glass had been swept into a corner with a piece of cardboard. A fresh-looking towel hung over one of the windows. In the kitchen, a new space heater was plugged into an extension cord which traveled out the window and into the weed-filled backyard. From there I presumed it met another cord, and eventually plugged into someone else's outlet one or two doors down.

"They were definitely here, and definitely had some money they didn't spend on crack."

"What's upstairs?" Mike asked. Two bedrooms, as it turned out. One had a bed of sorts, made out of clothes and blankets and two couch cushions piled artlessly against the far wall. Across the narrow hallway, the other bedroom was almost entirely empty. In it, leaning up against a wall, was Bernstein's Tower painting. "They're probably out shopping for a frame," Mike said.

"Asshole," I said.

"So, we can't stay. You're—"

"A person of interest in a murder case, yes, I know. That's why I let you drive me out here instead of just dropping me off at my place, so I could get my own car." But staying would have made sense. Mike would get bored and wander off, I'd have the place to myself, and I'd wait for Dad to come back with Grandma, grab her, and go. Unless Dad was armed, or his girl was, or he whored Grandma out, or killed her, or left her at a hospital after getting her to sign some papers. My mind spun with the possibilities, and all I could see before me was the Tower falling, and me buried under a thousand tons of steaming rubble.

Mike snapped his fingers in my face. I grabbed his wrist and locked it hard. Dad had showed me that one, in the old days. Mike's foot left the floor as he staggered in my grip. "Who the fuck do you think I am?" My voice was fried, a thrash growl. "Don't you fucking snap your fingers at me. I'll make sure you can't call the cops." Then Mike shoved me, but I held on. He regained his footing and rushed me against the wall. I got a knee up and he winced, but didn't drop. Wasn't this just like the left? Always at each other's throats? Mike grabbed my wrists now and tried to pin them against the wall, but I squirmed out and got a thumb at his Adam's apple, then hit his balls with my knee again, and shoved him away.

"Fuckin' crazy bitch," he said, best he could between coughs and spasms.

"Petit-bourgeois dilettante," I said, and that really hurt him. I marched past him, took the painting, and headed back downstairs. He called after me, "You're in my custody!" He even dug his car keys out of his pocket and jingled them. "I have the car!"

There is a feeling I've experienced only once or twice on my many strolls. *Waldeinsamkeit* is the feeling of being alone in the woods. When I was a kid, the whole area was wooded, except for Nesconset Highway, Route 25A, and Main Street. It seemed wooded anyway. My mother used to take me on strolls through the woods along the edges of the highway. Everything was amazing. The leaves under leaves, moldering and turning brown. The tall trees, and the ones that grew in large Ys or that shot out of the ground, practically horizontal. The malevolent-seeming poisons ivy and oak that she was so good at spotting and that I never even found until my ankles and shins burned. We never encountered another person on our walks, but I did encounter plenty of their spoor: beer bottles, condoms, once much of a car's shiny chrome bumper. I'd wanted to take it home; like a lot of kids I was obsessed with finding things, and selling them for big money. Even base metal could be transmuted into gold. US Steel was the biggest and most important company in the world, or at least it was on the television news every night.

Once we saw a turtle and she stood with me for ten minutes to watch it cross the little path we were walking down. Another time we saw a skunk and Mom made a game of walking slowly backwards, with exaggerated "ballerina steps" to keep us from getting sprayed. When we came across a recently dug hole, she told me that a leprechaun had dug it and that if we came back at the right time, the leprechaun would be there and give us ice cream. It took me weeks of begging and sniffling to get another trip to the woods, but by the time I found what I thought had been the clearing with the hole in it, the hole had either collapsed or been filled in.

Then came the bulldozers, and the strip malls, and the McMansions, and cancer, and almost all of the woods around Port Jefferson was gone. There was just enough for a few warrens of brown rabbits, and just enough for a girl to get lost in. That was me. I'd never experienced *Waldeinsamkeit* with Mom—by definition since I wasn't alone in the woods, and had never been as a child. And years later, when I began my strolls to just get out of the house, or to practice smoking, she was still with me, in my head, a Holy Guardian Angel of sorts warning me away from the poison ivy.

The only other time I'd experienced the strange wonder of being alone in the woods, of being alone in a world the edges of which only birds could perceive, was sometime prior to my first encounter with Bernstein. It was a night walk, in summer, and I'd taken a small bag of oranges with me to eat. The citrus was supposed to keep the mosquitoes away, and it almost did. It was a sticky night, but cooler outside than in the house. My parents never liked air conditioning; my mother used to say using it when the temperature was only in the eighties was "putting on airs." Then she'd giggle at her own pun. Also, my father was such a fuckup with money that we could have AC one week, and no power at all the next.

I made a few turns through the trees and almost sprained my ankle when I tripped over a root. Then I found it—the spot in the woods where there was no light pollution from the highway or the King Kullen supermarket, where the distant roar of the traffic was swallowed by the chirping of the crickets. And there were fireflies, and a dark and musky smell, like that of an animal that had never been bathed by human hands.

I started crying on the spot; it was so beautiful. I had the world all to myself, like I'd always wanted.

Now, I had Bernstein's painting. I followed the extension cord from the kitchen into the yard, and laughed when I saw that it wasn't connected to anywhere. Dad must have given up when the task of stealing electricity for Grandma turned out to be marginally harder than it seemed. The usual. Then I went into the woods. It was a bright day, and chilly, and soon my breath was steaming in front of me as I picked my way over the cracked and fallen trees left in the wake of the hurricane. There was plenty of noise from "Western Civilization"—what was Gandhi's line about thinking it would be a good idea to try it one day?—the blast of the ferry horn out on the Sound, a motorcycle roaring by, even a loud soap opera as I passed by one of the better houses. I was careful to make sure the painting wasn't scratched by the twigs I was brushing past, but I still felt it. I looked up at the sun and the blue-white sky and realized the awesomeness of the world. *Awesome* is a word that is tragically misused, especially on Long Island. It basically means "Oh boy!" among my age cohort and anyone younger. The notion of *awe* has been shorn from it. That's late capitalism for you—taking the sacred and transforming it into the profane for the sake of profit. There is nothing we're supposed to be in awe of, except for the *Batman* movie. But I was in awe of the wood through which I was traveling, which I was occupying like a tiny army. Small as it was, constrained as it was by highways and vinyl siding, these woods were something different, something real. And Bernstein would never see this again. I couldn't bring him out here and try to explain what I'd felt, even though I knew he'd just chuckle and then tell me of some greater experience he once had, likely involving the Great God Pan or a protest against clear-cutting. Or my grandmother could have been wandering through here a little while ago, finding a thin line of trees and following them to a greater wood in which to really get lost, confused and lonely and never to experience even a moment of *Waldeinsamkeit*. Someone was going to pay.

There was no satyr in these woods, and a moment later I heard some yelling in the distance. Just the sort of casual autumnal shrieking of a child on his bicycle. The feeling was gone. Some of the blue paint on the corner of the frame had flaked off onto my palm.

# 14.

I made it back to the apartment, and picked up what needed picking up. It wasn't that messy after all. We didn't have much, and my father had taken all he could carry. He probably had had that woman with him, or perhaps even a third person, and a car. One big trip and he took half our belongings. He left the TV, but the remote was missing. I imagined Grandma grabbing it in her claw-like hand and refusing to leave without it. My own overnight bag I'd left in the trunk of Mike's car, so I was down to a Hefty bag and an oversized purse for packing purposes. I found a jar of peanut butter, unopened, and a table-spoon and packed that as well. Then it was out to the Volkswagen. I smeared some mud over the license plates, then drove through the giant puddles in the Meat Farms parking lot to splash more dirty water along my wheels and the sides of the car. It was all busywork to keep from thinking about what I should have been thinking about—did Bernstein really kill himself? Did he "create" Chelsea on some level, transforming her into someone rather like me . . . or like he had wanted me to be? How long would it take for Dad to get sick of Grandma—I was fucking sick of her—and leave her in an ER somewhere, or even just on the side of the road? I'd been tempted to, but I needed her Social Security check to pay rent.

I am not a very nice person sometimes. I guess I do take after my dad.

I drove to the deli, bought a pack of cigarettes—Pall Mall Gold, like Grandma used to smoke before her dementia made that an arson risk—and dialed the hardcore show hotline from the pay phone outside. Another Abyssal Eyeballs show, but in two nights. I'd have to check that out. Then I drove into Joshua's development, parked about a block from his house, and walked the rest of the way. I waited for him on his stoop, smoking cigarettes and occasionally repositioning the painting on the step for it to be nonchalantly discovered next to my knees. I should have worn a skirt, but Joshua already had a masturbation problem and I needed his help.

The sun was down, and I had smoked four cigarettes, by the time he pulled up in his driveway. He had a bag of Chinese food with him—enough for three people from the look of it. "Hey," I said to him, "is it D&D night?"

"What do you want?" he asked, all surly. He stayed by the car, keys in hand. I waved my hand in the air to signal the motion detector porch light, then nodded toward the painting. "I brought something for you to look at."

Now Joshua was interested. "Where did you get that?"

"Oh, this ol' thing," I said. "A few places, actually."

"The Tower," Joshua said. He trotted up to the stoop. My stomach growled loudly. I was half-ready to trade the painting for his egg rolls.

"I was wondering if you could help me sell it," I said. "You must get a lot of freaks—uh, I mean, aficionados—in the store."

"What's its provenance?" He put his sack down, extracted from it a little white cardboard box and a plastic fork. No chopsticks for this guy. He ate his chow mein noisily.

"A semifamous occultist painted it."

"Some longhair's been looking for you," Joshua said. "Metalhead kid."

"Did he say what he wanted?"

"Nope," Joshua said. "Do you think I'm crazy? Why would I bother trying to sell some painting for you?"

"Can you afford a home in Port Jefferson on a comic book store clerk's salary?" I said. "No. You have sidelines. Selling stuff, probably. Porno Japanimation, other things, under the table. To weirdoes."

"Maybe I inherited this house."

"You didn't inherit shit."

"Yeah?" he said.

"Yeah—if you had, you would have sold it and moved away. That's what everyone your age, without kids, does. You know that Long Island is a little turd hanging off the east end of America."

"I'll be right back," he said. "You stay here. Give me the painting."

"I'll stay here with the painting."

Joshua dug his keys out of his pocket, which required some juggling of the chow mein and his bag of food—he held the latter between his fat knees—and muttered, "Excuse me," like he didn't hate me and I wasn't practically trespassing, and headed inside. If he called the cops, I'd jam. If he called anyone else, I'd be eager to see what they had to say for themselves.

I was surprised when, a few minutes later, a dumpy-looking station wagon pulled up behind Joshua's car. The door behind me swung open and Joshua stepped out. He smelled like food, and the sort of sour sweat typical of him. I was dazzled for a moment when the driver of the station wagon hit her high beams, and then when the lights went out like extinguished matches, out came Aram and Karen both. Karen smiled when she saw me. Aram had a camera with an unwieldy looking flash attachment.

"Well, hello!" he said. "We meet again. Are you the artist?" Without waiting for an answer he lifted the camera. I lifted the painting and interposed it between the lens and my face, and tried to tuck my knees up behind the canvas as well.

"I'll hold it," Karen volunteered. She stepped forward and plucked the painting from my hands without any other comment. She was tiny enough to hide behind the canvas for real, and she expertly kept her fingers off the painted surface. Aram grinned and took three photos. The flash filled the front yard of Joshua's house like a nightclub strobe light.

"Are you interested in buying this or no? It's not a tourist attraction."

"They represent . . ." Joshua said slowly, "a certain interested party."

"Aram's a Maugham scholar," Karen said from behind the paper. I did not know that.

"I'm mostly interested in Maugham's views of the Brontës, but I have a secondary interest in the Gothic, of course," Aram said. *Of course*, like I was another graduate student and not a punk kid, genius notwithstanding, who hung around Stony Brook mostly because they had shows there, and a cool radio station, a few real leftists—a short list from which I could now scratch the Red Submarine crew—and some people around my age I didn't want to brain with a hammer. But I knew enough to ask:

"Ah, so like *The Magician*, W. Somerset Maugham's book about Crowley." I instantly hated myself for adding *W. Somerset* to Maugham's name. It made me sound like I'd just read the name on the cover of the book and knew nothing else about him. Which was true, but to tantalize these people I had to come off as something other than a student. "Have you read much Crowley, actually?" I asked.

Aram smiled. He had so many teeth, it was almost inhuman, and they all appeared to be shaped exactly alike. "Oh no. I flipped through some of it; seemed like the rantings of a madman, which I'm sure Crowley in a lucid moment might admit that they were."

"Well, that's part of the charm. So, who are these photos going to?"

"Someone Aram's working with for his dissertation," Karen said.

"He might wish to buy the painting. How much are you asking?"

My mind buzzed. What's a deposit and a month's rent on a studio apartment around here? How would I even find a studio apartment around here, in prefab town? The East Village, maybe—no, that was a total fantasy. "That's negotiable," I said after too long a silence. "I'd have to meet any potential buyer. It's an occult thing; you wouldn't understand."

Aram chuckled and shrugged, like a cartoon bear. "I'm just a humble go-between," he said. Karen stiffened up though. I stood up and took the painting back. "But perhaps he would like to meet you. He's the sort of person who likes to . . . "

"Collect people," Karen said. She smiled again, this one forced, like a puppet built with posable lips. "In a good way. He's very wealthy, and occasionally even generous. He likes to have bohemian friends; he probably thinks it puts him in touch with a more authentic self."

"Something like that, yes. We'll get him these photos," Aram said. To Joshua: "We can contact you, yes?"

"I'm brokering any sale, yes," Joshua said. I put a dumb look on my face. I nodded at Joshua, and even beamed. Yep, just a girl with a ridiculous haircut, needing the comic book store manager's help to do anything more complicated than tie her shoes or suck a dick. "Bring the painting inside, Dawn," Joshua said, all nonchalant.

"I need to get it back home," I said. "I'll see you later, Josh." And with that I trotted away from the stoop.

Aram called out, "Can we give you a ride anywhere," and Karen giggled as I held the painting over my head and squeezed through some shrubbery to cut across a neighbor's backyard. Joshua just said *Shit!* and loudly.

I got to the car, started it, and was shaking almost too much to drive. There are no coincidences. There are no coincidences. And what did Joshua want with me, inside? Had he called the pigs after all, and let one in through the back door? Was he just going to cold conk me, tie me up, rape me? He'd probably jerk off to that little fantasy once he got over his disappointment, and his inability to chase after me. All men are pigs. I felt like a pig just for imagining Joshua's fantasies and so transparently getting them right.

I cut through the side streets and found the highway. It occurred to me that I had nowhere to go.

# 15.

In the city, homeless kids group together and live in squats, or in the park, or wander the seemingly endless labyrinth of the subway system. In the city, there are public bathrooms everywhere if you know which restaurants and bars to patronize, and there are tons of free food for the salvaging if you don't mind stale bagels and the occasional tussle with a rat. In the city, people don't lock their doors and call the cops when they see someone they don't like walk down their block. The entire system of telephony would collapse into a flaming wreck, sparks raining from every transformer on every telephone pole in the five boroughs.

But Long Island was not the city. It was where people went to escape the city, to free themselves from their kin and fellow ethnics, to play lord of the manor over their quarter-acre backyards. When Robert Moses had the Northern and Southern State Parkways built—the so-called "Master Builder" did not "build" them as historians and journalists would have it;workers build things, labor does—he kept the overpasses low to keep city buses, and blacks and Latinos, out of his island and off his precious Jones Beach.

Bernstein had had a great rant about Robert Moses, and made me read *The Power Broker*. "Unelected power, entirely occulted, and I mean that in both senses of the word, Amaranth!" he said as he handed it to me. He'd still occasionally call me Amaranth when excited, though by then he knew my name was Dawn. His other nickname for me was *Golden*

Dawn, which amused us both, but him much more. Robert Moses, despite his Jewish background, was a Freemason and had an abject fascination with the Aryan race. With Long Island as a mystic laboratory, Bernstein said, Moses wanted to bring a new people to a new promised land—WASPs. And he wanted to seal them off from the rest of the state of New York, in the hope that the lily-white Methodists and Presbyterians would, like millions of churning spermatozoa, alchemically and spontaneously generate a "social homunculus" that would have all the attributes of Adolf Hitler, save one: a human body. The body was the role of the mother, and in Moses's formulation, the phallic island had no yonic counterpart. And it happened too! Despite Nassau County having plenty of Jews, and Suffolk a huge Italian American population, the social homunculus was alive and helping drag the state of New York, and by extension all of America, to the right. "By the dawn of the new millennium," Bernstein told me, "fucking *Ayn Rand* will be considered a serious philosopher. Democrats will be pulling off shit that Ronny Ray-gun wets the bed dreaming of—slave labor for welfare mothers, permanent military bases all over the Middle East, torture chambers deep underground, bugs in every phone and office fax machine, computer chips in everything else, and robotic stealth bombers doing all the dirty work. And that will be the *liberalism* of the epoch. What Robert Moses summoned cannot ever be banished, not now that the Eastern bloc is in disarray, with the blood sacrifices in Tiananmen Square. There's some Taoist alchemy for you."

Bernstein rarely drank anything but water and Coca-Cola, and he finished a half-full two-liter bottle in an extended guzzle. Some trickled down his chest and belly. It had been a hot night, that one, and we were both sweating out our lusts for one another, in bed, me between his thighs as he declaimed. His balls tasted like sugar. Then he said, "Plus that fucker Moses chased the Dodgers out of Brooklyn. I'll never forgive him for that shit."

The Dodgers reminded me of an old 1010 WINS radio commercial. "Are the Dodgers coming back to Brooklyn?" the excited voice-over artist would shout, and the camera itself would zoom toward a clock radio. And WINS, a news station, reminded me of the newspaper, and that Dad used to buy *Newsday* for me to flip through when we went to the diner, even though we already had home delivery. There was a diner out in Hauppauge, open twenty-four hours a day. The Pioneer. I headed west, pleased to stop short of the city. *Wir bleiben hier.*

I got a booth in the back—the hostess was happy to oblige, given my looks—and bought a coffee. Bernstein had trained me to sit with my back to the wall whenever in a restaurant and to keep an eye on the entrance and windows. On the rare occasions when we went out to eat together, we'd share the same side of the booth. Waitresses often assumed that we were just high, or retarded. Once, I complained to Bernstein and he said, "Well, if that's what they think, they're half right."

I ordered a plate of fries, and read yesterday's paper, which someone had left behind in the booth some hours earlier. More enthusiasm for the crumbling of the Eastern bloc. Honecker was cornered by his party's own youth brigades, who chanted, "Gorby, help us! Gorby, save us!" What a pair of slogans—as if Gorby would do anything for those kids but hand them over to the West Germans so they could compete against Turkish immigrants for the lowest-paid work. We can only ever save ourselves, either as a class or as individuals.

The diner was mostly empty, but amazingly I saw someone I knew from Port Jefferson. It was the old Greek lady, with the cats. She was sitting at the counter, her legs not even touching the floor, and chatting amiably, in Greek, with the counterman. I had a reason to drive twelve miles, and past two or three other diners that actually close at one in the morning, but what would she be doing here? I studied her closely. She wasn't smiling. Both she and the counterman were Greek, but outside of a passing physical resemblance there was no sign that they were related. She was easily thirty years older than he, and wearing widow's black, so I wasn't witnessing a flirtation despite the occasional shoulder squeeze and loud laugh. She was old enough to be free of the tyranny of men. When was the last time I talked to a man who didn't want to fuck me, and the last time I talked to a woman about a subject other than men? Years, probably.

I inhaled deeply and concentrated. I raised my own feet from the floor, crossed my legs, shifted my weight onto my left side like the old woman did. I held my mouth like she did, drank the bitter remains of my coffee to match the tiny cup of the Turkish stuff she had before her. It was both sympathetic magic and basic materialism—by somatically emulating the woman I could gain entrée to her thought processes. I'd be her doppelgänger.

She was lonely. She was attempting to be an enthusiast to keep the man's attention. She knew that a tangle of ethnic, generational, and gendered obligations would keep him rooted on the spot, here and now without the excuse of other customers, chatting with her. That's why she drove twelve miles for a cup of midnight coffee. The alternative was home, and the cats, and a television full of people rapidly communicating in a language she still wasn't comfortable with. She liked feeling intelligent and rarely had the opportunity anymore. Once or twice in just a few minutes she corrected the pronunciation of something the counterman said—his

Greek wasn't native; the accent didn't sing. The counterman would have greatly preferred to speak in English, and she knew it, so exercised her power over him by sticking to Greek.

And I became her. I was lonely too. There was no place for me to go; I had no connections with anyone anymore, other than those I made by force. I felt like a tiny brain floating within a disobedient blob of a body, my protoplasm smeared against a corner of the Earth's rocky crust. But don't two smears grow closer and closer under the light of the sun, and finally become one? It was night out, but the moon was full and something quaked in my body and I decided to go for it. She would have something to teach me, this woman.

Finally, the counterman made his excuses and left his position. She held her posture and watched him slip into the kitchen, then immediately deflated. I took my coffee and walked up to her and said hello. I did it in that nonthreatening way people around here often do: "Hullo."

"Hello," she said. "Are you a clown?" There was no venom in her voice. She even smiled. She had a gold incisor. Total rock star. But she thought I might work at the circus, which might be in town, and after a long night of spritzing myself with seltzer I came to the diner for a late-night meal.

"No, I just like this look," I said.

She glanced up at the sides of my head. "Don't you get cold? Winter is coming?"

"I have a hat," and I produced my longshoreman's cap from the pocket of my jacket.

"Good, good," she said. "If your head is cold, everything is cold!" Then she said something in Greek. It sounded like *cot-zeh*. Then she said, "Sit, sit," and patted the stool next to hers. So I sat, and made a promise to myself not to speak of men. Of course, as the only thing I could think to ask about

was the counterman who had just left, I had efficiently
rendered myself a mute. The scars on my stomach tingled.
There was no need to worry, however. The woman was full
of conversation. She didn't even ask me my name, but offered
hers. She was Chrysoula. She said it meant "golden treasure"
and even tapped a fingernail against her tooth. Chrysoula
had a younger sister whose name I've forgotten, but it meant
"silver," and the economics of it all really tickled Chrysoula.
She said that she had seen me around Port Jefferson, and was
surprised to see me all the way out here, but she didn't ask
me what brought me to this diner, and didn't offer a reason
for her own patronage, except that the Lite-Haus Diner, in
Port Jeff, was disgusting and full of roaches. I mentioned that
my grandmother had once said the same thing, having seen
a roach there twenty-five years ago, before I was even born.
Then she launched into a long history of that diner and its
various owners, and their battles with both rats and health
inspectors. They had not acquitted themselves well against
either foe.

Here is the important thing that she said: "Watch out for
your family."

"My family?" I hadn't realized we had been talking about
family.

"The family is the problem," she said. "They're always
close. Too close." The counterman came back with a small
plate of greens, and two slices of lemon. Chrysoula dug in
without a word to him or me. "I am old, so nobody young
pays attention to me. A woman, so no man pays me attention
neither. Not American, so the Americans don't see me. But
I see all of them, you see?"

"I do see," I said. "So, you've seen me around? My family?"

"I see everything," she said. "I know your father. He walks
around the town on drugs." I instantly wanted to vomit. I was

tempted to ask if she had seen a lady even older than her wandering the streets of downtown Port Jeff in a pink housecoat, but thought the better of it. I liked this woman. She reminded me of me. "You come all the way here from Port Jefferson like me. You want to hide, but you are too crazy looking. Who are you hiding from? Where is your family, that you come to the diner so late at night and don't eat nothing?"

"So," I said, remembering my vow and nodding toward the little plate before her. "What you got there?" Talking about family would mean talking about men, necessarily.

Her mouth half-full, Chrysoula bared her teeth and said, "*Vleeta.*"

The counterman said, "It's amaranth. Greeks eat it. Sometimes hippie weirdoes do too." He shrugged. "It's just a normal green. Has sort of a sharp flavor." Bernstein used to call me Amaranth. There are no coincidences. I realized where my grandmother might be.

It wasn't a long drive back to Mount Sinai, but it felt like I was crawling along the asphalt instead of riding in my car. Every traffic light was against me, and I was at war with myself, as usual. Not just between the poles of attraction of Marxism and magick, but between my affection for my grandmother, my hatred of my father, and the fact that the old Greek lady was absolutely right. For all my posing, I was still a slave to my family and their demands. Bernstein was a respite from all that, or so I'd thought, but he was somehow attached to my father. My grandmother even had a nickname for him, one that she remembered. The fucking bat had been slipping up and calling me by my mother's name occasionally for the last six months. We had never looked alike, my mother and I, even before the Mohawk and the nose ring. But Bernstein she remembered.

I cut the lights and drove the car onto the side street and then onto the grass by the edge of the woods. I was pleased to have a tiny Rabbit, and found some shrubs behind which to park it. *Please please please*, I said to myself, my brain a big empty echo chamber. If there was no God, and there is no God, who was I saying please to? Molecules in motion, who had no interest in me. My Holy Guardian Angel, whom I'd never really heard from. To myself, hoping that I'd be wrong.

I grabbed my flashlight from the glove box and set off toward the ruins of Bernstein's house. It was getting cold these nights, and I couldn't imagine Dad really taking care of Grandma effectively. He might have just dumped the body there—*please please please* I said again, and then comforted myself by saying that I only didn't want to have to encounter a corpse and get mixed up with the police again—or left her there shivering and pissing in a corner. I left my flashlight off; I wanted the advantage of surprise. *Please please please* I wanted to be wrong about the whole thing.

There aren't many animals left on Long Island. The occasional deer, rabbits, sometimes a skunk or a raccoon, and those last always seemed surprisingly huge. Bernstein told me once that he had encountered a fox. There were certainly no predators worth worrying about, but when I heard a rustling amidst the trees, I flipped my flashlight on and gave it an arc-like swing. My father, a cop, the satyr even.

It was huge and white and reached out for me and screamed, limbs thrashing and blind. The air smelled like shit and rotten teeth and then it was on top of me, twigs gnarled up in its hair.

"Grandma!" I said. She slapped at my face, jammed a finger up my nose somehow. "Enough!" I managed to get my arms around her and then we both tumbled to the ground. I rolled over to pin her, and she cried and wailed. I grabbed a handful of leaves and shoved them in her mouth to keep her quiet. She tried to bite me, but her dentures were gone, so it was just a gross gumming. I balled up a fist and raised it high, but realized that I was thinking like a movie. Knocking someone out is never so clean in the real world. Nobody else seemed to be coming from the trees, and after a moment Grandma quieted down. I petted her cheek and even put my thumb back into her mouth to dig out the leaves. Her breathing was shallow, but steady.

"Why don't you come with me?" I said, softly. I had no idea where we would go. Back to the diner, maybe, to get her washed up, or maybe we could risk the apartment if I stayed up all night and sat with my back against the front door. She shook her head and, eyes wide and white, turned her head to look over to the ridge. Beyond that was Bernstein's cabin. Grandma's fingernails were all blackened, and chewed up. The crazy old bitch had probably scaled the ridge. She found the dirt and sank her fingers into it, clutching the earth.

"Fine," I said. "Stay here." She'd either follow me, in which case I'd head toward the car, or stay where she was, which was fine with me, or run off screaming again and I was pretty sure I could find her now that I knew that she was still alive. I figured that my father was down in Bernstein's cabin, hiding out from random imaginary enemies and going through the wreckage to see if there was anything salable.

I put my cap on my head and slowly eased down the embankment, then circled around to the side of the house that was still staved in from the tree. There was someone inside, but no flashlights, no loud noises. Just black-on-black shadows and familiar-sounding murmur. I knew it. *Agios, agios, agios.* Then a screech from inside nearly had my skeleton tearing itself out of my flesh.

"This isn't working!" It was Chelsea, hissing in a rage. Then I heard my father's voice saying, "Shut the fuck up!" between clenched teeth. I'd heard that before. I still couldn't see a thing, but I knew what they were doing. A Gnostic Mass, or parts of one anyway—it's not like a crackhead has the mental discipline for one, and there were only two of them poking around in the dark. Chelsea was naked, and shivering. I could hear her squirming on the filthy floor, her teeth chattering like die being cast from a cup. I was gladder than ever for my longshoreman's cap.

A moonbeam showed me a flash of thigh. She was crawling out from under Dad; he was all ribs and broomstick limbs. "You promised!" she said, and she squirmed out of his grip, and her robe, and smacked him across the face. "You said you had money, that you had power. That you could do things!"

Chelsea was my doppelgänger, as though cloned from my blood and soul. For a moment, I wanted to cry. I remembered the moment my father had finally betrayed me with his incompetence so well. And it had nothing to do with Mom's death, or crack, or anything so melodramatic. It was a slow grind through childhood. A layoff from Grumman here, an obviously ripe piece of bullshit spilling from his mouth there, telling all of his friends that of course he was voting Reagan in '84, but confiding in Mom that he was going to secretly pull the lever for Mondale—all that stuff. Then he kicked himself off the cliff one steaming July day back when I was a knock-kneed kid who liked Duran Duran and pink bubblegum. I'd been out riding bikes with neighbor kids or something asinine like that, and when I got home I found him on the couch, alone, eating an entire pizza, from local favorite Carnival Pizza. Dad was in his underwear, and his belly was slick with pizza grease. It was too hot to eat, really, and Dad was making eating pizza look like something dirty and weird, but I loved Carnival and I wanted some. So I said, "Oh boy, pizza! Can I have a slice?"

With his mouth full, Dad said, "Fuck you." He swallowed and added, "Get your own." Then he practically shoved an entire slice into his mouth, puffing out his cheeks like a fat child in a bad movie. I almost vomited right there. Ours was a household where it was a big deal when Mom said "damn," and Grandma used to stretch out the word *suuuuugar* to keep herself from saying "shit" in front of me.

Finally, I said, "I'm gonna tell—"

"Shut the fuck up," my father said. I ran outside, tears everywhere, and got back on my bike and rode around the block two dozen times till my calves screamed. I was wishing that a car would come out of nowhere and hit me, then I'd have to go to the hospital and I'd be in traction, wrapped in mummy bandages. Dad would be sorry and Mom would make him buy me a whole pizza, and he'd have to feed it to me.

Nothing happened. I eventually went back home and never mentioned the pizza, or Dad's outburst. The next day, he brought me home a model ICBM from work. It was a fun toy. Dad had worked on the guidance system, so I enjoyed playing Ronald Reagan. I'd press the imaginary Red Button and hoist the missile into the air, announce that its gyroscopes were going crazy and sending the warheads right into the White House, leading to a planet-incinerating chain reaction. *Pcchrrruu! Kra-kraaaa-throoooom!*

I always was a bit of a tomboy. When Dad started telling me to study hard at math so I could go to work for a defense contractor too, I decided to focus on my diary and bullshit teenage poetry instead.

And now, years later, a girl just like me, but skinny and thus better, crawled out from under my father, and she was

crying just the way my father used to make me cry, too.
She wasn't Bernstein's. She was never Bernstein's. She
was always my father's. I burned with jealousy and rage.
That great dark thing was rising again up from the center
of the Earth, but I didn't feel it pushing up through my
spine. It was without, away from me. The night went dark
again as a cloud ate the moon, and Chelsea said, "O Lion
and O Serpent that destroy the destroyer, be mighty among
us!" There was a rush of movement, thrashing about. I so
wanted to turn on my flashlight, but there were two of
them, and something else huge and coiling about the little
building.

Chelsea said it again, that line from the Gnostic Mass: "O
Lion and O Serpent that destroy the destroyer, be mighty
among us!" And my father just laughed. That cruel laugh.
The wind picked up and sent the woods talking.

Maybe she should have said that line a third time, and
offered her breasts to my father, the priest. "You promised,"
Chelsea shouted. "You said! I shaved my fucking head for
this. I had to deal with your crazy mother to get us to this
point too. Who the hell brings their mother to a thing like
this? What were you thinking?"

"Oh, you got a better plan for money than her?" my father
said. And like that, the coiling dark dissipated. He was no
magus; he was just another low-level grifter looking to cash
in on an old lady's Social Security. And not a very smart one,
because he brought her around while he contrived to fuck a
teenage girl who dressed just like his own daughter. "Forget
it, bitch," he said. "Nothing's gonna happen now. You're just
shouting at a big old empty universe full of shit, you understand? Do you?"

And there Dad was, wise again. The universe is empty,
with nothing left to grind against but itself. What remains is

Qliphoth, those rotten poison husks. Waste products of creation. Cosmic shit.

Chelsea and Dad were both completely wrapped up in one another, able even to stand naked in the autumn cold, fuming and steaming and screaming at one another without noticing me a few yards away, on the other side of a shattered wall. I could have walked between them and waved hello and they wouldn't have perceived me. That was good. They didn't want me, and they only wanted Grandma for her money. But there was something else they wanted. I lifted my feet carefully, walking backward as best I could in the dark and mud. Whatever they wanted, I wanted it too. And I'd trade Grandma back to them for it if need be.

Grandma had made it to the lip of the ridge by the time I got back up to it. She was utterly covered in filth, and that made the decision for me—we'd go back to the apartment, keep the lights off, and hope the police didn't come sniffing around for a day or two. She looked up at me and smiled and said a name. Not *Dawn*.

"Chelsea." And she smiled at me.

# 16.

Grandma's dementia wasn't so far gone that I had to bathe her regularly. Normally, yelling at her to go take a shower would work. She had never even had a broken hip. But that night she was a wreck. I put her in the back of the car, and she managed to flail about so much that I could hardly see out the rear window, it was so streaked with mud. I stayed off Nesconse Highway as much as possible, to avoid the cops, and let her burn herself out with the yelling for a doctor—"I can't breathe! You're trying to kill me!"—and for Chelsea—"Sweet, sweet Chelsea, why are you treating me like this all of a sudden?"— before bringing her upstairs. Then she was pliable enough to manhandle into the tub and scrub clean. Her body was a torn and deflated balloon; it made me want to die.

I was never straight edge. It always seemed cultish and stupid—not like Thelema or Trotskyism, she said ironically to herself. I just never drank much because of Dad, and thanks to my late poverty. If there was ever a time for a beer and some television, this was it. Bernstein would have snorted. He always said that TV was just like Buddhist meditation, except that the focus was on samsara. It drained the Will, and replaced it with bourgeois propaganda via teletrancing. Grandma couldn't afford cable, but there was one beer left, and so it and a freshman DJ on WUSB stammering her way through a 3–6 a.m. shift kept me company.

So, Bernstein and my father had been school chums. My father had some knowledge of the occult, probably thanks to

Bernstein and old Black Sabbath LPs. Dad had never really
fit in with the grownups on the block, I realized now. It's
actually hard to get laid off from a defense contractor—well,
until this summer. With the deformed and degenerated
workers' states on the verge of full capitalist restoration, the
bourgeoisie are already talking about a "peace dividend," as
though they wouldn't just find some other enemies to target.
But all Long Island is fearful now. *What if nuclear war isn't
inevitable? How are we going to pay down the mortgages on
our homes?* That's the logic of the middle class.

My father was always just smart enough to see through the
bullshit, but not smart enough to do anything about it. He had
been an engineer, and to hear him tell it he was a good one.
But engineers are never any good at working with people, so
he was always being outmaneuvered, blowing up at his
bosses, and getting shitcanned.

"Even with science, it's all about sucking cock," he had told
me, with my mother dying in the hospital bed between us. I
was visiting, he had just stormed in, his tie in disarray. "Cock!"

"Fired again?" I said, softly as possible, willing him to
quiet down. Mother was on a morphine drip at this point, so
she was feeling no pain.

"Fuck it, Dawn. Mama's more tumor than woman," he said.
He leaned down and spoke into her mouth. "You win, you
fucking cells. No more job, no more insurance. Enjoy your
last meal, tumors!" He put his head into his palms. "Laid off
again. I did all the work, solved all the problems. The stellar-
inertial guidance system works thanks to me; otherwise our
fucking missiles couldn't hit the ocean! But some stockholder
wanted his nephew to have a job, and . . ."

"Dad, you have to—"

"What?" He looked up at me. There was no sadness in his
eyes, and not even rage. Just pure terror. "Get another job?

Yeah, I can do that. I'll just go down to Sperry . . . Oh wait, there's no more Sperry. *Unisys.*" He hissed that last word. "Except," more hissing, "they're leaving the island."

"So, let's leave the island!" I said, though of course Mom couldn't survive any move. She couldn't survive at all.

"We are staying here!" he said. And he was right. Mom died soon enough, and he went crazy.

And now, Dad had apparently found Chelsea somewhere, convinced her to adopt my look, and was fucking her as well as his regular crackhead girlfriend. She called the pigs on me in the hope of giving Dad a chance to kidnap Grandma. Chelsea had some big dreams of magick, but crack had long ago ruined Dad's Will, to the extent that he ever had any.

Did Dad kill Bernstein? Did Chelsea? Why? Certainly not for money. I wouldn't be surprised if Bernstein had been loaded, but a clever Marxist like him would know all the capitalist tricks—trust funds and Swiss bank accounts, beachfront property on islands just big enough for a post-colonial flag, shares in thoroughbred horses. The instruments of capital proles like me only ever hear about thanks to stuffy, snooty characters on television sitcoms.

Once upon a time Dad would use the stars to chart the course of world events—that is, he designed celestial guid-ance systems that sent missiles to rain down fire and death upon the masses who dared cross his masters. It was almost like magick. Now he's just another crackhead, and Chelsea was stupid enough to go along with whatever schemes come out of his dead gap-toothed mouth. The plan might have not been much more than "Get Dawn out of the way, grab Mama, fuck in the ruins, then move into the apartment and wait till the first of the month for the Social Security check." But they wouldn't be fucking in Bernstein's house, or be interested at all in him, without somehow having something to do with his death. I surely would have noticed my own father, who was never subtle, sniffing around Bernstein, and Bernstein would have said something.

No, he wouldn't have. He never explained that he had known my father, and my grandmother, back when he was a high school kid whose abiding interests were Black Sabbath, model airplane glue, and painting. Yes, the Tower painting was important too somehow. The situation was too much, the time so late, the—

No. Not right. I am a fucking genius. What was required was a change in perspective. The situation was extremely simple. There were five billion people on Earth, but only a minute number of possible suspects. And it wasn't late; it was early. The sun was just a few hours from rising. I was spending too much time and energy trying to outguess a moron and a psychopath, and not nearly enough focusing on my goal. I turned off the TV. I got up and poured the rest of the beer down the kitchen sink.

*Dharana* yoga is the meditation of concentration, one I was never very good at. Think of a red triangle. That's it. It's one of the four hardest things in the world. One thinks of a red triangle, then of the person who told them to think of a red triangle. Of a red triangle, then of a slice of pizza. Of a red triangle, then of gravity's pull tugging one's ass toward the center of the earth. Of a red triangle, and how hard it is to keep thinking of a red triangle. Of a red triangle, and of the old canard that it's impossible not to think of a white horse on command. And that's the first several seconds.

Bernstein smiled at me once—a wide smile, that revealed a dead, gray molar—and told me that the secret was to actually think of a five-pointed red star. The red star of the working class ascendant. The five points representing the five fingers of the worker's hand, through which all wealth is created. The five points representing the five continents, the whole wide world that the worker has to gain.

"Seven continents," I said.

Bernstein scowled. "What's a continent and what isn't is a matter of cultural and ideological imperatives—much of the world counts only five continents. Here in the US we keep seven, because of racist antipathy toward Latin America, and because of colonial designs on Antarctica. Think of the Olympic flag. Another symbol. Five rings for five continents."

"Oh," I said. Another factoid to file away.

"Back to the red star. The red for militant struggle—as opposed to the yellow hammer and sickle that represented labor at peace. Peace that floats in a sea of red blood," Bernstein said.

"That sounds like a lot to think about," I'd said. "Isn't the idea to think of one arbitrary thing?"

"There are no arbitrary things. Exoterically, sure. Logos—" then he stopped, and laughed, and started again. "Logos are not *logos*," Bernstein said, interrupting himself, saying *logos* with a soft *g*, like the Greek word. "See, there's one now. Yes, logos are just often arbitrary-seeming symbols, but there are layers of esoteric truth in every curve and corner of a design. Draw a circle in the sand around a lone rock and someone will worship it. What is it the Firesign Theatre said? 'There's a seeker born every minute.'"

I remembered rolling my eyes. "Now you're just babbling."

"Am I?"

"Well . . . oh, of course." Then I got it. Another lesson from the magus, this one via negative example. "All those were your 'breaks'—what you found yourself thinking of instead of thinking of a red triangle. A red star, I mean."

Bernstein held his smile, which made me melt. He usually just flashed a smile, and snickered like that old cartoon dog

Muttley. "And I had a realization. The red star is five red triangles. It was like a factory speed-up. I got down in twenty percent of the time most seekers do." Then he laughed at his own joke.

So I sat and thought of a red triangle, then my mind drifted back to Bernstein and the conversation. So I decided to move on to the red star, which brought me to mind of Tiananmen Square, and the victory of the bureaucracy over the incipient revolutionaries back in the summer. What would happen now about capitalist counterrevolution? In twenty years, China would be another Japan. And the Eastern bloc, and glasnost, what would become of the degenerated and deformed workers' states of Europe? The whole of the epoch filled my head. Everything was in a state of collapse: my own life, the entire system of the world.

I caught my breath, and almost got up to stick my head into the sink and lick the beer droplets left on the drain. But then I realized what I needed to meditate on. The Tower painting. More complex than a red triangle, but that would make it easier. There was always more tower to envision, always more collapse to embrace. When a tower collapses, all of it falls to the earth, eventually. Flying, screaming people, the great clouds of dust that shoot into the air and cover the sun, the flames that rise high and burn out—we're all ultimately headed straight down. I would have gone to the car to get it, but I was too exhausted. If Dad, or whoever, swiped it again, they could have it and sell it. I concentrated on the painting till every stroke was tattooed on my brain. I owned it now; it was mine, forever.

# 17.

When the going gets tough, the tough go punk. The Abyssal Eyeballs were playing that night. A part of me realized that it would be just too neat if Chelsea appeared at the show, perhaps with my father or Greg in tow. Or if Aram and Karen showed up again, with a name and phone number for the person who wanted the Tower painting. At the same time, what else could possibly happen?

The day was long. Grandma was covered in bruises and whimpering in pain like a dying puppy. I had to carry her to the bathroom and then back to bed. She wouldn't sleep, or eat, robbing me of my occasional standby of slipping her an over-the-counter antihistamine crushed up in a jelly sandwich. She didn't eat peanut butter anymore—dentures, you know.

"What happened? What happened?" Grandma kept saying. "Where's Billy? I lost Billy in the woods." She asked me, "But you were there. You must know where Billy got off to. Why don't you tell me?" She cried till her tear ducts dried out, and gulped water like a child.

"Chelsea . . ." She called me Chelsea. I almost slapped her right in the mouth. "You have to understand something about Billy. He doesn't always think clearly. Sometimes he says things that, at the time, he thinks he will do, but then doesn't do it."

"I know, Grandma," I said.

"I don't know what happened to him. I don't know what I did wrong. He was a nice boy, a good boy. Always very attentive. It was when he got married and had that baby that something turned in him. It was like he expected to be a teenager forever, Chelsea. No wonder he likes you so much."

I doubted that there was any percentage in pretending to be Chelsea, but there's even less in arguing with dementia. "Does he ever talk about me?" I tried.

"Oh yes, all the time," Grandma said. I knew that was a delusion. Grandma hadn't said more than a hundred words to my father in months. Grandma continued,. "He says you're very smart and do well in school, and that he met you at Good Read Book Stop, and that's how he knew how smart you were."

I supposed it was possible that the bookstore could be a lead. What else did I know about Chelsea? She was fucking my father. She owned, or had access to, a Volvo. I hadn't known her in school, or even seen her around, so she was probably from the Village, not Port Jefferson Station— different school districts. Probably some rich bitch out for a few thrills. Maybe she'd been to the bookstore.

Grandma was telling me a story about how smart I was. How an essay I wrote was published in the elementary school newsletter back when I was in second grade. No wonder my father made his teenage girlfriend shave her head so he could fuck a girl who looked just like me. He surely missed me very much. Grandma's story ended, "And then Dawn brought home the newsletter and said that she had her essay in it. And that's how I knew she was so smart. One time in second grade . . ." She looped through the story again in its entirety.

"We're going downtown," I announced suddenly. Grandma was startled. Her lip started trembling. "No arguments. Billy lives downtown, don't you know?" I couldn't leave Grandma alone; who knows whom she'd let into the house while I was out. She fussed, but was interested. I got her into her housecoat and packed a bag. I told her it was in case we got lost, which she was addled enough to believe. I locked up the apartment as securely as I could and drove right to St. Charles Hospital. I walked her into the ER, and she followed silently until she saw the check-in window.

"What are we doing here?" she whispered to me.

"You're covered in bruises, Grandma," I said. "Look at your arms!" They were well marked from last night's exertions and a couple of days of rough living in squats and who knew where else. Then I whispered, "I think Billy knows who did it. I'll find him and bring him here. You just stay here, and let the doctors take care of you." For a second I thought she might begin screaming, and bring the orderlies down on us. Then I'd have to fill out forms, answer questions about her physical condition, perhaps submit to a police interrogation. But she was tired, and had burnt herself out this morning. I sat her down, handed her her bag, and said I was going to get a doctor. Instead, I left. On the way out I passed an orderly and asked for the chapel, telling him that I wanted to light a candle for my grandmother, at whom I pointed. Grandma even waved to me. Of course, I looked just like the bride of Satan, so the kid mostly just stammered and blinked before waving his arm in the direction of the chapel. I asked him to keep an eye on her, and he shrugged and said he would. I whispered that I thought she had tried to commit suicide—instant bump-up on triage that way—and split.

I didn't know what I expected to find at Good Read, but I had little to do before the Abyssal Eyeballs show, which was being held in a secret location. Sounded promising. Before Bernstein, Good Read was my education in both magick and Marxism. It's a used and antiquarian bookstore, the sort of place where one could buy a sack of paperback horror novels for a dollar, or spend five thousand bucks on a signed first edition Nabokov. Cool stuff, and a great way to peer into the collective psyche of the older generation and the way they used to live, and think, before they all sold out and went to work for Grumman or the state.

The section on Marxism and anarchism was a mishmash of old party pamphlets—Maoists of various stripes, mostly, as the specter of a black boyfriend was most offensive to parents back in the sixties—anti-Communist exposés from the fifties, a lot of stuff on economic calculation and planning, anarchist classics, and some scholarly material. But it was enough for me. The occult section was similarly a dog's breakfast: UFO abduction stories, Seth books, Edgar Cayce, some pagan junk, and some actually cool stuff. Maybe Satanic boyfriends were even more fearsome a generation ago. My first ever occult book was the hysterical *The Magick of Chant-O-Matics* by Raymond Buckland. One of the chants literally went, in part, "Now, now, now / money, money, money!" Funny, my father used to mutter exactly that, all the time, under his breath.

And as though the thought made him materialize, the chimes rang as he pushed the door open with his shoulder. It was Riley, the man from Belle Terre. He had a big cardboard box in his arms, and struggled with its weight. I slid behind a shelf and thought of nothingness—much easier than trying to think of nothing. The clerk didn't smile at him, but his eyebrows went up as he got to the counter with a single lurch and plopped the box on the table.

"Well, this should do it," Riley said. I'd never heard his voice before. I had no idea what I expected him to sound like, but whatever it was, I was wrong. His voice was deep and soft at the same time, like a crooner from a black-and-white movie. "A free trade between fair traders." I wanted to strangle him. Bernstein was always of the mind that the capitalists knew the score, that Communism was inevitable, but Riley spoke like a bourgeois economics textbook.

"Okay, we'll take a look," the clerk said. "Take a *look*." The air turned dark and cold, like a meat freezer's. He reached in and pulled out a few slim, but wide, volumes, bound in leather like new library books. The spines were unremarkable, but familiar all the same. There's no reason to print a hundred-page poster-sized book unless there are lots of images, diagrams. Art books, technical manuals, heavy math shit, and occult texts. That's where I'd seen them. Bernstein's house.

"Those are mine," I said as I stepped out from behind the shelf. "You stole them from my friend." Riley smiled at me, but didn't say anything. He didn't look surprised to see me, or upset. That was the archconfidence of the ruling class. Reagan and Bush smiling at the television while the Eastern bloc imploded.

The clerk shrugged. "I'm not interested in buying stolen merchandise," he said to Riley. And then he turned to me. "Do you have any proof that this is your, uh, collection?"

"You should ask him for proof that they belong to him," I said. "Those are valuable books. You could probably buy a house from the proceeds. If I pointed to an empty house and said, 'Hey, it's mine. Wanna buy it?' would you without seeing a deed?"

"What do you know about these books?" the clerk said.

"What do you know about deeds?" Riley asked.

"Magick," I said. "Sacred geometry, summoning spirits, enlightenment. Not the junk you can find at B. Dalton either. The real shit."

"You're right," Riley said. "These are occult books. But you're also wrong." The clerk put the books back into the box, planted the frayed elbows of his sweater onto the countertop, and rested his chin atop his knuckles. He rarely got a show like this.

"Here's how you're wrong, miss," Riley said. "I can point to a house and say, 'Hey, it's mine. Wanna buy it?' as you put it, because I own a significant amount of real estate in the Village, and in Port Jefferson Station as well. Point in any random direction, and you'll likely be pointing at one of my properties. There have been a fair number of short sales lately, foreclosures. Don't you read the papers?"

"Which suggests to me that these very expensive books do belong to him," the clerk said. "He can afford them, and we've been arranging this barter for months. This man knows their contents. Do you?"

"I know many things," I said. I pointed at Riley. "Have we met before?"

"Of course not," he said. "We clearly don't traffic in the same circles," he added, as an aside to the clerk.

"Clearly," the clerk agreed.

"Then how do I know that your name is Riley?"

Riley jerked back, surprised, but the clerk shrugged and said, "Maybe you do read the papers. What are they calling you these days, Mr. Riley?"

Riley regained his composure. "Mr. Peace Dividend." He smiled at me, the way a dentist does to a nervous kid. The worst possible smile. "I made a fair amount of money betting on war, in the markets."

"How many millions of dollars' worth of Grumman stock did you own?" the clerk asked him, fawning.

"More than enough. Too much, truly," Riley said. "I liquidated it, decided to get into real estate. Then the East Germans developed a taste for freedom. I got out of the stock market just in time."

"And you also dabble in the occult?" I asked.

"I 'dabble' in commodities. I can't make heads or tails of this stuff, and that's because there's no heads or tails to be made of it. Occult books, fine art, palladium futures; it's all the same to me. That's my business. Now why don't you mind your own business and let us carry on."

Then I performed a bit of magick I'd never been able to. I started crying, at Will. Real tears. The tension fell from my face, my skin heated up, my voice changed to the sort of girlish coo I didn't know I was capable of. "You don't understand," I said. "My life is really falling apart right now. I lost my boyfriend—these are his books, or he left them with me. And now he ran off with some high school girl. LILCO is going to cut the lights." I blinked away the tears. "I don't even know why you're picking on me! What have I ever done to you?"

It was good. Almost all of it was true. Riley was impressed, but all my body did was stiffen a bit, against his own Will. But he wasn't the target; the clerk was. If he shipped them out of town, I'd never see them again.

"Mr. Riley, do you know what this woman is talking about?" the clerk asked. He seemed dubious about the whole thing. The store was still cold, but now the frost seemed to be coming from his icy exhalations.

Riley made an uncomfortable little noise. "I'm afraid I do. If you're concerned, just hold the books for now."

"Oh, I'm not concerned," the clerk said. He ducked under the counter and brought up a large, soft-looking package in a plain brown wrapper. It wasn't a book, whatever it was. "Here you are, Mr. Riley." Riley hugged the package to his chest, squeezing it almost comically, and without another word left the store.

I turned off the tears. "What was in that package?" I asked the clerk.

"Are you a police officer?" he asked. "Or are you just insane?"

"No. Would you tell me if I were?"

"Insane?"

"No, a police officer."

"No, I would not tell you either way," the clerk said.

"It was in a plain brown wrapper. Was it porn? Kiddie porn?" He opened his mouth to say something but I interrupted him, because men hate when women interrupt them. "No, it wasn't even a book. It was a blow-up doll, wasn't it? Maybe a kiddie-shaped blow-up doll." I was close to shouting, "Pedophilia!" *Pedophilia!* was a powerful magical word, the *abrahadabra* of the late twentieth century. It shattered lives and tore up schoolyards in the search for secret sex tunnels, it pit neighbor against neighbor and legalized murder. *Pedophilia!* was a summoning word, a whistle for Satan and his army of prick-dicked imps. It could set a suburb to boil. Even I was a little wary of saying it too seriously, though if I could have done it, I would have won far more easily. *Pedophilia!* and the cops tear Riley's mansion apart. *Pedophilia!* and Joshua gets dragged away, blubbering that he will tell who wanted Bernstein's painting, and that sexy Japanese cartoons are too a legitimate art form. *Pedophilia!* and Dad goes away for a long long time. Maybe forever. But I couldn't say it; I wasn't even as good a witch as the girls from Salem. A failure of my Will, a reminder of my father and his living voodoo doll of me, Chelsea.

"Why don't you go ask him," the clerk said. "To be perfectly honest, I don't even know what's in that package. I just midwived the exchange."

"Didn't you care at all?"

The clerk looked at me, his eyes wide and hollow. He clearly didn't care about anything. That's why he chose to work in a used bookstore in a town where people rarely read anything more challenging than Danielle Steele. "Fine, then," I said, and I left.

"Hello! Riley?" I called out, on the street. He was only half a block away, headed down the picturesque little hill that made the block so attractive to day-trippers, and already had his car keys out. His *Mercedes* keys. I clomped after him, and he was being all cool. He didn't turn around when I called his name a second time. He was so good at ignoring people. I let him get into his car and drive off. He made a left at the end of the block, suggesting that he was headed home. I could head over there myself pretty easily. Maybe I'd even see Chrysoula sweeping up after him, or cutting the crusts off his bread.

"Riley!" someone else called out. It wasn't me; it was another woman, one with a familiar voice. I turned to see— it was Dad's crackhead girlfriend, tumbling down the block behind me, hissing and growling. She walked by me, calling for Riley, ignoring me utterly.

I wanted her attention. "Hey, bitch; get any dick from my father lately?"

"No," she said. "Haven't you?"

"What do you want with that guy?"

"Maybe I want to suck his dick because your father turned out to be a faggot."

I shrugged, and tried not to laugh. "I guess that's a strong possibility."

"What's your problem, bitch?" she wanted to know. All curious, almost like a normal person. "I need money, and he has it. He owes your father money, which means he owes me money. You too, you fat fucking bitch, but I know you don't have shit."

"How does he owe my father money? That guy's rich." It was probably a mistake, listening to this woman's hysterical babbling.

"From high school. They went to McDonald's every day and ate Big Macs. In college, your father was a real fucking sport and bought all the beer for their little faggot parties. That's how! Two hundred dollars," she said, her voice a shriek now. "With interest! Compound fucking interest."

"You've got to be kidding," I said.

"I was there with Billy. I saw it all," she said. "You think I've always been like this? You think I like living in a fucking abandoned house and shitting in the backyard? I went to school, you know, and I have a degree, so I'm fucking better than you. And I've got your father back, too. He came crawling to me when that whore he married finally fucking died." She stared at me hard for a long moment. I guess she could have head butted me if she wanted to, if she had the balance to pull it off. Then her rictus broke, and she was afraid.

"What's so funny?" she asked me. She was quieter now. "What's so goddamned funny?" She wouldn't even say "fucking" to my face anymore. I hadn't even realized it, but I was smiling at her.

Lots of things were funny. My mouth was open, ready to announce the punch line, and even explain the joke. Whatever I said was going to be true. I had thought that I was a member in good standing of the Imaginary Party. Chairman Bernstein, Comrade Dawn. But something wicked this way had come, and neither of us had suspected at all. It was as though everyone in this stupid town was involved in a conspiracy except for us. Riley had Bernstein's books; my father knew Bernstein too. And Riley bragged about buying up real estate—he was obviously the third friend my grandmother had mentioned, the one who bought the house out from under us. And now, here was Dad's crackhead high school girl-friend, looking for Riley. I couldn't ask any more questions of anyone. That would simply summon more doubt into my reality, bind my seekings with confusion. But I had no conclusions either, so I could say nothing. But I could still make a definitive statement.

I glanced around to make sure nobody was watching, then punched her in the face with every ounce of strength I had. It was a very good punch. I turned my ankle, loaded up my thigh, kept my arm all loose to get the kinetic link to my leg muscles going, focused on the first two knuckles, the whole Mike Tyson bit. I felt like there was another me, my own executive function or Holy Guardian Angel, observing from several feet away, critiquing my form. And my form was good. For me, the punch was a moment that stretched; for her it was a flash of flesh and pain, as it should be. Her nose vanished under my fist and her eyes glazed over. When I pulled my fist back—I was ready to unload a second time—she stood in front of me for a long moment. Then someone pulled the spine from her body and she crumpled to the ground, nice and easy. It was a mercy, really. Now she wasn't all frantic about getting her hands on crack. With that nose, she wouldn't be sucking dick behind the bait shop for five dollars a go for a few days anyway. I was practically a social worker. And I wasn't even wearing my spiked ring.

By the time I made it to Belle Terre, it was getting dark. I was mostly keeping an eye on the sun, as it was a long walk back to where I'd hidden the car after leaving the hospital. Grandma was probably being treated very nicely at the hospital. She liked pudding. The lights were on in Riley's home, and his wife was in the living room reading a magazine on the couch, but Riley wasn't anywhere to be seen at first. Then I noticed a light in the basement window well.

I had to scuttle up to the well on my belly to see into the depths of the basement. It was huge—a single room the size of the manse—and finished. And Riley stood before a lectern. He wore a gaudy robe, black with pentagrams stitched in sequins, over his street clothes. Riley looked ridiculous, like the milquetoast boys Molly Ringwald woos in the movies with her eccentricities and spastic dancing, ten years later. Like a second-string Nazi. He hadn't even taken off his sweater for the ritual. His pits must have been hot and stinking.

I presumed that the robe was his latest Good Read purchase. There was a book on the stand—it was an old book, definitely. Not even early twentieth century, nothing mass produced. The walls seemed to be lined with similar spines. Nothing I recognized from Bernstein's, except as a matter of type. One corner was stocked with different books, thick and shiny volumes of your everyday law library. So Riley *was* an occultist—and even worse he was an attorney—and his sanctum was a furnished, carpeted basement with a relatively high ceiling and an old wet bar in the corner.

I wondered whether it was selling his soul to the most foul and darkest power that made his fortune, or if he used magick. *Now, now, now / money, money, money!* Riley didn't seem engaged in a ritual. He was just skimming the book, turning a page every few seconds with gloved hands. Then I heard a dial tone, and static, and some buzzing. He had a PC with a modem in his sanctum too, and it was probably in one of the corners by the well, so I hadn't spotted it. Riley pulled his gloves off as he marched toward the computer, toward *me*—I rolled out of his line of sight, then rolled back after a moment—and began typing in a noisy clatter. I couldn't see him anymore though, as he was tucked away somewhere against the wall. But many things were explained. At least one thing was. Surely, Riley was the collector looking to buy the Tower painting. He seemed like that kind of idiot, trying to buy magick instead of earning it.

And he was rich. And he was an occultist. Bernstein's rival, revealed at last.

# 18.

So, did Riley kill Bernstein? On one level, it hardly mattered. His neck was made for the lamppost. That he was a practitioner made him fit my mental profile of who might have killed Bernstein, but the world couldn't wait for him to hang even were he innocent. Nobody gets as wealthy as Riley without exploiting the working class. That said, I was no anarchist. Killing an individual capitalist brings us no closer to revolution, and only leads to state repression. What did Trotsky say? *If it makes sense to terrify highly placed personages with the roar of explosions, where is the need for the party?*

But the great dark thing welled up in me again, filling the empty space behind my eyes. It was a roar in me, and I nearly threw myself in through the window, head first, to scuttle along the floor and kill Riley with my teeth. Then I realized something: I'd only ever attacked people weaker than I. That poor woman, damaged and enslaved by society and patriarchy. Joshua, a declassed, fat loser. Even idiot Greg. I've never taken on anyone who I thought, even for a moment, that I couldn't beat. The black receded into the bowels of the Earth, and I had nothing left to do but run.

I was only halfway across the huge yard when a flashlight beam cut across the night before me. Chrysoula, in her widow's black, held the torch and ran the light over me.

"Ah, you," she said. "What are you doing here?"

"Oh, I know Riley. My father does, I mean." Of course, that was true. In their youth. Occult shenanigans. Something.

"Your family," she said, her accent thick on her tongue. "Your father. Yes, I know him. He walks around town, your father."

"What are you doing here?" I said.

"I'm looking for a cat," she said. I found myself wondering if she was looking for a missing cat, or if she was just looking for a brand-new cat to bring home for her collection.

"Well, I should leave you to it," I said.

"Why? Where are you going now?" She stepped up to me, aimed the flashlight at my face.

"I put my grandmother in the hospital today. I have to go visit her. Some bad things happened to her—there are people in this town interested in beating up older ladies, so watch out."

Chrysoula shifted the flashlight in her hand, holding it like a club. "I'll beat them down."

"Well, okay!" I went to move, and Chrysoula went to step in front of me. Then light flooded the lawn. Riley's Mercedes roared past us. I thought I saw that he was still wearing his robe. "Did you see that?" I asked. "Do you know about your boss?"

"He's not my boss. I'm my own boss."

"Do you know what he does in that big basement of his?"

"I don't clean basements, or bay windows." She was about to say something else, when a cat emerged from the shrubs, ran over to her, and began rubbing its flanks against her ankles.

"Well, so glad I could be here for you," I said. "Goodbye!" And I ran as best I could in my big boots.

Everything was coming together and falling apart at once. Revelations led only to further mysteries. Was there anyone in town not connected to Bernstein somehow, not part of his life? I thought he belonged to me—after all, I belonged to him, and wasn't it mutual, contractual? But everyone had a piece of him, it seemed. My father, Mike Schmidt, Riley, Grandma. Everyone in town was part of the Octopus of the occult, cadre of the Imaginary Party, and I was the outsider.

I was used to being an outsider.

There's a trick to it. To be an outsider means to be connected to the inside somehow. It's a dialectic, or *taijitu*— the symbol beloved by kung-fu weirdoes and van art aficionados, with the white spot in the black fish, and vice versa. An outsider is more than a stranger, less than a friend. We cannot help but be inside everywhere. And I was headed in deeper than I'd ever been.

The night was a cold one. There was even a layer of frost on the Rabbit's windshield when I got to it. I spared a thought for my grandmother, then realized that I'd probably never see her again. I sure as hell wasn't going back for her. She'd never find me. I couldn't imagine her getting down to Riverhead, or wherever I was going to end up after the quick if sensational trial, to visit me on the other side of the reinforced glass. Tonight, I had nothing to gain but my chains.

On the drive, I briefly considered saying *fuck it* and pointing the little car toward Manhattan. A kernel of a plan came to mind—go hang out at CBGB's or ABC No Rio. Find some dude. Fuck him for a place to sleep and some cigarettes. Get a job at a restaurant, maybe off the books or with lots of tips, and then just live. Forget Bernstein; he sure as hell wouldn't be searching for my killer. Forget the remnants of family; they were eager to forget me, either through drugs or dementia. I had nothing else out here. Long Island isn't built for anyone over the age of seventeen and under the age of thirty-seven. Even the college kids at Stony Brook are mostly commuters, filling the LIRR with dirty laundry and Brooklyn accents to head back home to the city every Friday.

But no. *Wir bleiben hier.* We are staying here. Manhattan wasn't a Big Rock Candy Mountain with nothing to do all day but hang out in Washington Square Park and wait for Joey Ramone to show up with a free pizza. It was Wall Street. It was Central Park West. The Twin Towers. The very center of world capitalism. With the implosion of East Germany, it was only a matter of time. The little nooks and crannies in which people like me dwelled, in shitty roach-strewn tenements with bathtubs in the kitchen, were about to be gentrified, or torn down completely and utterly replaced by condos for the children of the bourgeoisie. There was no place for me in the city.

Long Island, thanks to the summoning spell of Robert Moses, was static. It would always be like this, half-formed and stupid. Like me. I turned the wheel and headed back to the apartment, to pee, to eat something. *I'm a person of interest*, I thought to myself. Beyond a mere murder investigation, I was a person of interest to the entire town. There was something in the air, a charge. I was the lightning rod.

When I got home, there was a letter waiting for me. It hadn't been mailed. There was no stamp, and no address. Just my name in someone's idiot scrawl on a small envelope, embossed with a rose. A mother's stationery set. I opened it and read a very brief note, from Greg:

> *Dawn,*
>
> *Rodrick told me not to leave a massage on the phone answering machine so I am writng this. Your friend "Mike" "the Communist Layer" called me when he could not call you to tell me to tell you that your grandma's old house is now owned by Galt Omni Limited Holding Company. Rodrick and I will be at Obissul Eyeballs and will see you there.*
>
> *PS: You were right about Chelsea. She's a skank.*

I'd figured the Riley connection already, and was only mildly surprised to see that Greg couldn't spell "abyssal." Or "Roderick." Or simpler words. He was a little shaky on what quotation marks meant too. Chelsea had probably dropped Greg when she realized that he wouldn't be a good way to get to me, but that was the least of my concerns now.

There's an occult joke in the phrase name Galt Omni Limited. Obviously Galt was a reference to Ayn Rand and her noxious fictions. "Omni Limited" is too dumb on its face to be anything but secretly clever. Riley had all but admitted that he owned half the town, so it was probably him. What made Rand's imagination "omnilimited" was her vulgar materialism. "Metaphysics: Objective Reality." That was Marx's error too, of course. He missed that the little bags of chemical reactions we all carry around in our skulls have perceptual abilities we haven't tapped yet. We could perceive abstractions—such as freedom, such as Satan—so thoroughly that we could bring them into existence. The lie that becomes the truth. If you're not willing to speak falsehood and lie in the same utterance, no, *as* the same utterance, your bold and totalizing truths will only ever be lies.

That's why Bernstein wasn't interested in money. He had plenty, somewhere. But he didn't play the game. He was afraid of it, though of course he never put it that way.

"There are many gods one can summon, Amaranth," he told me once. It was an unusual night. We actually went out for a walk through the woods rather than just spending the whole evening on his couch. "As many as you can fathom, and gods unnamed in deeper fathoms still. But don't waste what I'm giving you by summoning Mammon."

Inspired by another Deren film, *The Very Eye of Night*, we had walked out among the trees with no flashlights, under the dark of the new moon. The only illumination came from the far-off highway, and from fireflies. We wanted to walk among a field of stars, nothing but inky black and bright pinpoints. But it still smelled rich, fecund, and my lips were salty from the trek.

Bernstein's voice was disembodied; he was a black blob picking his way through other black blobs. "Ever read the New Testament? When I was young, I found it exotic, a treat. Finally, the protagonist of the Bible revealed!"

"Of course not," I said. "I've only ever read kiddie versions, or saw boring religious cartoons, or heard references or aphorisms, or memorized a verse or two for a lollipop. The wages of sin are death, and the wages of knowing that the wages of sin are death is a Tootsie Roll Pop."

Bernstein chuckled in the dark. I rarely got him to laugh, so I was secretly thrilled. "You might have heard this then: For where your treasure is, there will your heart be also. No man can serve two masters: for either he will hate the one, and love the other; or else he will hold to the one, and despise the other. *Ye cannot serve God and Mammon.*" He affected a Thurston Howellesque accent for the last sentence, and we both had a laugh.

"It's true, you see. Mammon is the magick that is the end of magick. You cannot serve any god and Mammon. You cannot *be* any god and Mammon." He smacked a bush and sent a swarm of fireflies into the air. "Every man and woman is a star," he said, mostly to himself.

"So, Bernstein, you agree with Judeo-Christian slave ideology. Ooh, the poor are special, the rich are evil."

"Judeo-Christian slave ideology is half-right," he said. Another truth—I'd been poor for a while. So had my dad, my grandmother, that crack whore I cracked open. There was nothing special about them, or me. I checked the fridge, but no food had magically appeared, nor another beer. All the

Will in the world won't fill an empty stomach. I was just another welfare moocher, not special at all, except for what Bernstein had taught me. I could be any god I wanted to be. I would be the god of the abyss tonight.

I didn't bother hiding the car a few blocks from the venue, or applying new mud to the license plates. Let the pigs tow the Volkswagen away; it meant nothing to me. I was staying here. Let them try to interrogate my grandmother again. Maybe her senile storytelling would work in my favor this time.

# 19.

Roderick was pissing against the side of a tree in a yard by the house. It was to be another basement show. I walked up to him and said, "Hey, nice cock."

"Thanks," he said. "I inherited it from my father. But if you want more than what you see, you'll need to pay me a quarter." He tucked it back into his pants and zipped. "I won't offer to shake hands with you."

"I appreciate that, thank you," I said. "So, getting a good crowd for the show?"

He nodded. "Yup. Should be a good one. Promises have been made."

"Do you know the Abyssal Eyeballs well?"

"Eh, not really," he said with a shrug. "But they weren't the ones to make the promise, you know?"

"I don't."

"You don't?"

I rolled my eyes. You'd think I'd be used to the utter absence of straight answers in my life by this point, but no, not really. "Is Greg here?"

"Yeah, he said he'd be here. Didn't he talk to you?"

I shrugged. "He left me a note. I've been busy."

"What have you been up to?" Roderick asked.

"I beat the shit out of some crackhead bitch," I said. "A girlfriend of my father's."

"A girlfriend? Does he have more than one?"

I nodded. "Yeah. He's a very attractive crack-addicted crazy person and incompetent fuckface who let my mother die because he couldn't even keep a job building nuclear bombs for Ronald fucking Reagan." Roderick sucked on his teeth, unsure. "You know, Reagan had a large appetite for nuclear holocaust. It should have been like selling shoes to socialites."

"Well, okay," he said. "Your father . . . Well, he sounds like a real piece of work. Anyway, let's go in. It's cold out here."

There was a cellar door, the good kind, the kind worth sliding down, and it was open. Some didgeridoo music floated out from its maw. We stepped into the basement and both of us giggled. The place had a nautical theme—very Long Island. Stuffed swordfish on the wall right over the slapped-together plywood and 2 x 4 stage, a pair of white lifesavers on the far wall, netting strewn with fake plastic starfish. The staircase leading upstairs into the home proper was decorated too, with fishing oars and boxes of tackle put on display under glass, like mutant butterflies. There was a boom box in the corner, and not too far from it stood Karen, leaning against a pillar. Even the pillar was decorated with some nautical knot work. She was the only one here, and so small none of us saw her until she waved.

"Hey," she said when she saw me. Her smile seemed authentic. "Did you bring the painting?"

"Why would I bring the painting to a house show?" I asked. It was in the car, but she didn't need to know that.

"Painting?" Roderick asked.

"Well . . ." Karen started. "I thought maybe you would. I mean, what else would you do with it? Where would you keep it now?"

"Now," I repeated. She had nothing to say to that.

So, "Hello, my name is Karen!" she said instead, turning toward Roderick, her tiny hand out. He shook it, confused. "Didn't you host the last show?"

Roderick nodded. "Yeah, I did. Kinda. I don't know the band at all, really, but I got an offer you couldn't refuse, let's say."

"Ah," Karen said. "Friends in high places?" She was suddenly suspicious. Then we all had an awkward moment.

Roderick said, "More like low places." He tapped the floor with his foot and winked at me.

I had no idea what he was talking about, and decided to go for it. "What do you mean by that? What are you talking about, Roderick? What's your connection to the Abyssal Eyeballs, to this house, to the people who are coming tonight? Do you know that girl with the Chelsea haircut?" He stared at me, and so did Karen. "She's fucking my father."

"She looks like you," Karen said.

"I know. That's purposeful," I said. "But Roderick, I was talking to you, about you."

"Well," he said, "I've got some cousins who work in construction and home improvement, so we know all the good basements—"

"And these events?"

Roderick snorted. "If I could explain these events . . ." He trailed off, waved his arms, then started again. "Well, you were at the last one." We were all agreed, at least if awkward silence equals vague consent.

"Look, there's a fake plastic seagull hanging from two wires in that other corner," I said, finally.

"I feel like I should have a kid's menu and a paper placemat with word puzzles and a labyrinth," Roderick said. "I want fish and chips."

"Where's Aram?" I asked Karen. Then I wanted to chew my tongue to pieces and spit it out. Asking about a man, again. The old patriarchal script.

"He'll be here soon," Karen said. And with that, our conversation was truly over. Neither of us had anything to say. We both turned to Roderick, but he was out of ideas as well. The door at the top of the steps squeaked open, then someone flicked the lights on and off. "Hello?" Karen called out, but nobody answered. The lights went out completely. The door shut. In a corner, the building's furnace roared to life, a little peephole of fire sending our shadows strobing against the walls.

The cellar door opened again, and down walked Greg on mantis legs. It took me a moment to see that there were other people with him; he was so tall compared to everyone else. With one step he broke from the pack and stood before me, expectant. Was he expecting a hug and a kiss? He said, "Hey, you're out. Was it that guy you made me call?" He put out his arms and really did hug me. I kept my hands at my sides. "I'm surprised. He didn't sound rich," he continued in a whisper, arms tight around me.

"Hi," Karen said. "You were at the *last* Abyssal Eyeballs show?" Roderick looked at Greg but didn't say anything.

"Anyway, he's outside," Greg said to me, in my ear. "He has a flier about you, but he wouldn't give me one. I think he recognized my voice." The basement was filling up now. It was larger than the last basement venue, and the Abyssal Eyeballs fan base had seemingly expanded over the last week to match it. Perversely, I wondered if Riley would host a house show of his own in that gorgeous basement of his, then I remembered that I might have to kill him somehow tonight.

The band had come in with the bulk of the crowd, sight unseen by most, but I spotted them. I pushed through the crowd toward the heavy woman, the beatboxer, but was intercepted by Chelsea. Another person I felt like killing.

"Guess what?" she said. "Daddy's mad at you." She laughed, a quick piping *haha!* and smirked at me.

"Why? Because I won't fuck him, so he has to depend on a skank like you? Should I let you know when I change haircuts so you can rush out and get one just like it?" I said.

"You know why," she said.

"Let him call the pigs," I said. "Hello, police? I'm a crack addict and I'd like to report a crime against my favorite crack whore. She's a little wary of coming down to the station to file a report for some reason, so could you send a couple of officers down to my crack-house squat?"

Chelsea cracked a smile at that, and snorted. "Cute. You don't even know what the hell's going on, do you?"

Something came up from under my feet. It was that black thing from the core of the Earth, more huge than ever before. An ocean-sized wave, filling me up, every cell. The band started with a deep bass roar that made my sternum vibrate. Everyone felt it, and shut the hell up. The Abyssal Eyeballs were all pro. No tuning, no fucking around with the monitors, no clumsy banter with the crowd or grumbling amongst themselves; they were on stage and making a joyful noise with a single depressed key on an electronic keyboard. Chelsea and I both turned to the band, though the only light was from the furnace, which was still grinding away in counterpoint to the deep note from the Abyss.

Chelsea leaned in and whispered in my ear. "You're gonna fucking die," then put herself back upright.

So I leaned in and said, in her ear, "No, you are."

It was a weird crowd, I realized as my eyes adjusted. Chelsea and I must have looked like foreign exchange students from another planet. And there was Greg, and Roderick, who was at least a kid, but everyone else was dressed like the bush-league bourgeoisie. Button-down shirts with pinstripes, Dockers, pencil skirts and blouses with the giant shoulder pads for the women, of which there were a few. Karen, who hadn't drifted from her corner—I realized now that she was in charge of the boom box and had turned it off at some point to wait for her next cue—looked practically homeless next to the women here.

So she was with the band. And had a contact with the would-be buyer of my Tower painting. Who was certainly Riley. Who knew Bernstein, and who bought the house out from under us. Who knew my father. My father, who was in the room. I didn't recognize him at first because he was in drag as a member of the middle class. I remembered that suit jacket, that tie. I'd bought it for him for Father's Day, with the few dollars I'd made from babysitting, back when people would actually let me near their kids. What little Daddy's crack habit didn't kill, my punk rock habit had. The band shifted toward a song of some sort—there was beatboxing, drumming, odd groans and noises, all on the lower registers. I was in the belly of a whale, a great leviathan. My father seemed caught up in the noise just as much as everyone else. Aram, a hulk next to Karen, was entranced. Greg peered up at some special part of the ceiling. And the people I didn't know, or barely did, from the bus or the mall or who were neighbors of my junior high school friends, were all one with the sound.

I felt it too, but I also experienced something deeper, more familiar. That great and dark sea under the sands of Long Island. It was both ocean and creature, a thing so huge it swam in itself. As the Abyssal Eyeballs played, a pair of eyes appeared before me. The Leviathan. *None is so fierce that dare stir him up: who then is able to stand before me?* Leviathan is older than all the old things. He is the one who cut this long island free from the earth; he is the glacier and we are just the moraine. The debris left in his wake.

And Leviathan looked at me, and Leviathan loved me. I

spent an eternity staring into his eyes, and he stared back into mine. This was the great Bernsteinian secret. The Leviathan, the great watery creature, he was the mystic incarnation of the mass struggle. The class, or nation, or race. Like the sea itself, Leviathan carved out the borders of the lands of earth, and we little monkeys could not help but fill the niches Leviathan left in his wake. Leviathan, all consuming, that was the god I would be.

"Bernstein . . ." I said, and though I whispered I was sure everyone heard me, and everyone knew of him, and everyone now understood him. This is what he had been looking for in the pages of *Workers Vanguard*, and in his brief trip aboard the Red Submarine, and in his endless rituals, the psychedelic experiences, the Hermetic experiments.

Water is cold and gets colder the deeper one goes. But beyond where men can swim, where the sheer fact of water is so dense we can not penetrate without crushing our bones and meatbags to jelly, water boils and seethes. In the coils of the Leviathan. The monster burned with rage. I knew the feeling, and I smiled. And I knew what was going to happen to me now. There'd be no j_____, but there would be vengeance. I would swallow Mammon whole.

The song stopped, and the lights flared to life. I already had my eyes closed. My father wrapped his necktie—the one I bought him, with horseshoes on it for good luck—around my neck, and Chelsea punched me in the stomach. There was a generalized cheer as I buckled over. The bitch had palmed a roll of quarters or something. Big Aram grabbed me by the shoulders and pushed me onto the little stage, and expertly tied the tongue of Dad's necktie around a trio of thin copper pipes running along the low ceiling of the basement. It was tight around my neck, but not too bad. I could even address the crowd, if I so wanted.

"Yeah!" Dad said. "Fuck fucking yeah!" He spun on his heel to get a good look at everyone, and to make sure that everyone got a good look at him. "See, this is going to happen, just like I said!" Chelsea twitched her jaw, contemplative. I glanced around the room myself, not looking for allies, but rather for reactions. Greg was pale, sweaty. He took a step forward, but some guy whose muscles showed like bowling balls under his preppy sweater put a thick palm on his chest and stopped him. Roderick was cool. He winked at me. Most everyone else was hungry for me.

Bernstein had never fucked me. My mouth, sure. Honestly, part of my attraction to him, part of why I kept coming around his little shack of a house in those early days was in the hope that he would. What would he be like in bed, for real? Would he close his eyes? Was he a chatterer? The type to say "Good girl" or just grunt? Were his chest and arms covered in scars from his attempts at *Liber III vel Jugorum*? Was he a condom fumbler or the type of guy to just pull out and come on my tits, then expect me to coo like some porn star?

Which I totally would have done for him, had he wanted to fuck me. But he didn't. Instead, we breathed together, adopted yoga postures together, and spent hours in these awkward positions, reading the sectarian left press together for kernels of Divine Wisdom together. And I sucked him off like I was a diabetic and his *ov* was insulin. I had a very strong jaw, and neck, thanks to Bernstein.

Dad started ranting, and gesticulating. Something about the "excess road to wisdom leads to a palace!" He hardly knew anything about magick; drugs had scrambled his brains as much as the ice pick had scrambled Trotsky's. But he had his Chelsea, who was smiling at me, like she was the flower girl and I was the bride, and this small crowd of people—

maybe twenty-five all told—were the guests, and they were rapt. I don't know if they believed Dad's shit, or just wanted to see a girl get killed, live and in 3-D. Fat Joshua from the comic shop had eased down the cellar door steps and filled up that little doorway. Mike was sharking his way to the front, cutting between shoulders with the palm of his hand. He made it up to Dad and squeezed his shoulder.

"This is fantastic. You're a fucking hero, man," he said.

"Yeah, I am," Dad said. "Now don't fucking interrupt me again." He looked to Aram. "Take him!" Aram actually did lurch over and grab Mike by the collar, but there was really nowhere to go in the overcrowded basement, so they both just stood there, looking stupid. I glanced back at Karen. She had a hand on her chest, and was rubbing.

Dad's valedictory didn't make much sense. He was a magus. I was a sacrifice. My blood would swirl down the drains built into the basement floor and feed the Great Thing on which Long Island was built. The capitalist system was working too well—the commies were running, collapsing like a house of cards and falling like dominoes, and wilting under the fires of superior productivity, and dissolving like rock in the pipe, and other clichés, and that was not fair. Not fair to anyone who had been told that their services were no longer required at Grumman, Sperry, Fairchild, all the defense contractors with local offices. *A peace dividend*, Dad snarled rhetorically, would just lead to *division* into *pieces*, and poverty for the assembled.

My father always had an air of rat-like charisma about him, and times were tough on Long Island. He could have sold insurance to teenagers with freshly minted drivers' licenses, or prime Florida swampland to seniors eager to follow the advice on the banners some guy had hung on overpasses: GET OUT OF NEW YORK STATE, BEFORE IT'S TOO LATE! Dad could have done a lot of things, but instead he did all this. A little cult of thirty desperate people or so. That's magick, and politics, these days.

"We'll all live like niggers!" he shouted. "You want that?" Dad demanded of one guy in particular, who was too surprised to answer. So Dad turned and shoved his index finger into someone else's chest. "Do you?" That guy just shook his head no, slowly and gravely.

"Because that's what I've been doing. On purpose! Living like a nigger. On Long Island, where there aren't supposed to be any goddamned niggers, I smoked crack! I sucked dick for five bucks a pop just to get another rock! I would have fucked my own daughter, just like those dirty niggers do!" He gestured at Chelsea with that revelation. She was stoic, smirking even. "I had to crawl down into the muck and horror of it all, to bring back the fire of wisdom, to understand what is to be done!" I could almost hear the capitals: *What Is To Be Done*, like Lenin's famous pamphlet.

"I'll kill my only begotten daughter, a commie and a whore. It'll all come back," Dad said. "Something else will rise in the East, *orientis*! And America will come crawling back to us," he said, his arms wide. "For her defense. Lady Liberty, on her knees like a whore, eyes wide and mouth open. She shall never raise her head from our laps again."

I looked over at Mike. He cringed and mouthed four words: *There is no alternative*. Packed with occult significance, that phrase was. Margaret Thatcher's line—*there is no alternative* to neoliberal global capitalism. *TINA*. Death to Communism, death to even social democracy and the welfare state. Death to society; there's no such thing as society anyway. Mike looked terrified. What would the yang of capitalism be without the yin of Communism to keep it in check, and to keep Mike's identity as a revolutionary intact and unchanging? There was no alternative to capitalism; we both knew that now, and for Mike there was no alternative save to throw in with Dad, against Bernstein, and join this fascist schism from the Invisible Party, and keep the red flag waving. No wonder he had wanted to keep an eye on me after coming to bail me out of prison. Hell, no wonder he had actually bothered bailing me out. Even Aram and Karen were slaves to the state. Without the threat of Communism, and the allure of radical chic, the state universities would have their budgets slashed, and ultimately they'd be privatized. There is no alternative . . . to having to go out and get a real job. *Good luck, English majors.*

I was suddenly very happy that Mike was standing next to my father, and next to Chelsea. I wondered if Chelsea's real name wasn't "Tina." These things have a tendency to harmonize.

But here's what Dad misunderstood. Everything was harmonizing around me, not him. I was the synthesis of Bernstein's thesis and his antithesis. He was summoning up that which he could not put down. This motley crew of accountants and academics and hausfraus would never be the revolutionary class—they would never be Leviathan. A cabal of idiot imps begging a greater God to intervene on their collective behalf? These fuckers should have just gone to church or something. Leviathan had been calling to me, filling me up, since Bernstein's death. Bernstein was the sacrifice for the summoning, and Leviathan was bound to me. There are no coincidences. Leviathan had brought these people here, on deep currents of magick and geopolitics, before me. I was on the podium; they stood low before me. I was the executioner; they were to fill the drains with their blood and fat, on which Leviathan would sup. Even the choice of a basement made it easier for me, for the beast under my feet. It was cold outside, but so hot where I was standing. Oh, that furnace.

I began *dharana*. The Tower. *Break down the fortress of thine individual self, that thy truth may spring free from the ruins. Quarrel, combat, danger, ruin, destruction of plans, sudden death, escape from prison*—his interpretation from *The Book of Thoth*. Crowley's Tower is not just struck down by lightning; it is consumed from below by the great maw of Dis. *All that is solid melts into air.* Dad's voice was a buzz, of no concern to me. It only took an instant for enlightenment to strike. The waters of the deep boiled under me, in me, over me.

Dad made a few more flourishes, then Chelsea flicked open a straight razor and handed it to him with a smile on her face. The rest of the crowd was serious.

"Wait, don't!" I said, holding out my hands. "No, please!"

I showed everyone my palms.

"Why didn't you chain up her arms!" Mike cried. "Christ, did you *lose* them?"

Nothing up my sleeves.

"Doesn't matter," Dad said. He stepped up onto the stage to stand right before me.

And now, the levitation trick.

I tensed my neck and jaw, and lifted my legs, tucking my knees under my breasts. It was hard. My throat clamped shut. Eyes bulged open. Hung in the air. Feet twitching. Dad threw out an arm to draw the razor. In the left. That *sinister* hand. Then Leviathan. It called to me, and I was pulled down to the earth.

*Abrahadabra!*

And the three copper pipes, thin hot-water pipes, on which I had been hanging, came with me. The solder on the seams gave way. Cheap suburban Long Island ticky-tacky shit. Dad ate a faceful of steam and scalding water. His nose disintegrated before he even started screaming, and his eyes were smashed to jelly in their sockets. Mike almost dodged, but one of the boiling streams pulled his cheeks from his skull and filled his mouth, and cooked his lungs.

And Chelsea, sweet little Chelsea who looked like a skinny version of me, whose lithe body—Daddy's favorite thing— wouldn't have sundered the pipes had she been the one hanging, had she lifted her feet—she went slow. She got a faceful of Job 14:20—*Out of his nostrils goeth smoke, as out of a seething pot or caldron*—but lived long enough to claw at her face and scream and spit teeth before running right into Dad's flailing arms, into the razor meant for me. The air was all steam and misty blood.

It all took less than a second. The crowd burst toward the doors, howling and throwing their limbs over their faces.

Aram made a mad dash for the razor. "No!" he shouted at the heart of the world. His Will rose up like a mountain pushed high with magma, and he would have slit me from throat to cunt, I know it, but for Roderick. He had one of the fishing oars from the wall and cracked it on the back of Aram's neck. Aram fell in front of me, and I looked up and smiled.

Greg was there too, with an oar of his own. "Uh, we should go!" he croaked out. "Heavy fucking shit!" I coughed in response and waved them away. Roderick held out a hand but I mouthed the word *Go!* And they did, cleaving a path through the last knot of evacuees. Greg nailed Joshua with a pretty heavy shot on his way out, and Joshua went down even harder, head first on the cement steps of the cellar. *One more thing for me to step over*, I thought.

I found a few valves on the pipes leading back to the furnace and turned them till the water stopped. I took a few deep breaths. It wouldn't matter if someone called the cops, or if they came. There was no place I could be locked up where my Will would not be free, where Leviathan would not be coiling and churning right under my feet.

But then, I realized that among the corpses of my enemies, one was missing. Riley. I palmed my keys and headed out to the Rabbit.

# 20.

Marx has a great line. It's so great, in fact, that it is often misquoted and misused. It goes like this: *Hegel remarks somewhere that all great world-historic facts and personages appear, so to speak, twice. He forgot to add: the first time as tragedy, the second time as farce.* Usually, people think it's just about history repeating itself, and not historical figures bubbling up out of the dynamic of the world to make a fool of themselves a generation or three after appearing so terrible. And there was Riley, appearing for the second time, in his magickal vestments, jimmying open my car's hatch.

"Hello," I said. My voice was fried. I felt like my throat had been balled up and left at the bottom of a laundry hamper, then quickly and incompletely ironed three months later.

"Hi," he said, with a wave and a nod. He had a leather portfolio case with him. The hatch finally opened and he removed the painting.

"That's mine."

"No ma'am," he said, smiling. "It's mine. I won it from a rival, long ago. Then lent it out, and it was never returned to me."

"I just killed three people, and I need some milk or something to soothe my throat. So put the painting down."

He did, but in a way that told me that he was planning on picking it right back up after our conversation was concluded, and bringing it to his Mercedes, which was parked just a few yards away.

"Oh, you're a killer, eh? Anyone I know?"

"I'm sure. My father."

"And he is . . . ?"

"Seliger," I said. "Also, Mike Schmidt."

"Ah yes, the Communist," Riley said, solemnly. "The other Communist, I suppose I should say."

"They were trying to kill me."

Riley unzipped his portfolio, turned it upside down, and shook out some imaginary dust. Then he smoothed over his robes, and gathered up the fabric to examine the hem. "No agent of the state can perceive me while I wear this," he murmured, mostly to himself.

"Have you tested it?" I asked.

"I've read the specs," he said. Then he turned back to me, smiling a Ronald Reagan smile. "Why were they trying to kill you?"

"I was to be a sacrifice, to keep the Cold War going, so that everyone could have cushy defense contractor jobs. They were attempting to summon Leviathan, I believe, but Leviathan summoned me to kill them."

"Well, you're a very lucky young lady, Ms. Seliger," he said. And he moved to put the painting into his bag. I grabbed the long sleeve of his robe.

"From whom did you win this painting?"

"Jerome Bernstein, of course," Riley said. Then, as if I didn't know, he added, "the artist."

"And to whom did you lend it?"

"To your father, actually. He thought it would help him with something important." Riley smiled. "His wife was ill. Was she your mother? I don't mean to pry. Divorce and remarriage are so common these days. Marriage is but a contract, and contracts are made to be broken."

"I thought they were made to be kept."

"Depends on with whom one makes them, I suppose."

"Yeah . . ." I said. "She was my mother. She's dead."

"I'm sorry to hear," Riley said. "But your father never returned the painting. Did he give it to you?"

"No," I said. "I found it. Some kid had it."

"Who?" There was an edge in Riley's voice now.

"Kid named Greg. Tall, blond. Dirtbag."

"Oh, I saw him run by," Riley said. "Were you trying to kill him?"

"No. But *he* had found it at a junk shop. The Greek Orthodox church one."

Riley muttered *Greek Orthodox* and slapped his thigh. "Oh, well, I suppose I owe your father an apology, then. I bet what happened is that he brought the painting back to my home when I wasn't home, and gave it to the maid. She was probably . . ." He stopped, and searched for a word. ". . . Perturbed by it and brought it to her priest."

"You don't let her into the basement, I know," I said.

Riley's smile twitched. I cleared my throat while he composed himself.

"I see," he finally said.

"What about your wife?"

"Oh, I'm not married. I do hire a woman to come in sometimes, sit around, eat a meal with me. That sort of thing."

"Weird."

Riley shrugged. He was very philosophical. I was actually enjoying this conversation. The Leviathan seemed to have retreated. I did not know how to kill this man.

"Well, it's good for men to have female companionship. There are many ways to get it. Offer money, love, power . . ." He glanced at the painting. "Why did you think the painting was yours?"

"I . . . Well, I thought my father was given it by . . ." I

coughed again. " . . . The artist. I knew the artist well. I'd go to his house, sit around, occasionally share a meal with him."

"Ah," he said. "So you knew Bernstein."

"I knew him. Very well, I knew him."

"It was a tragedy, his suicide."

"He didn't commit suicide," I said. "The gun was in the wrong hand. Someone killed him."

Riley shook his head. "His Will was his own. But you're very nearly correct in your suspicions. It wasn't an everyday suicide."

"What did you do to him?" I felt it in my stomach, in my throat. It wasn't the great deep thing, it was just plain rage and bile.

"Ms. Seliger," Riley told me, "I told him the truth. I initiated him into a higher level. He couldn't handle it. The truth . . . rewired him. Of course he shot himself with his off hand; his entire *Weltanschauung* had been inverted." He paused, then the smile returned, full force. "Do you know what *Weltan*—"

"Yeah yeah, worldview." I wanted to kill him, right here, but he was just so eager to share, so confident in his own powers, that I wanted to hear what he had to say. And also, I was afraid. Leviathan had receded into the dark waters underground. It was just me now, a girl with half-assed understandings of both magick and Marxism, against Mammon.

"Close enough. He and I have worked together for a long time. He was a fucking *genius*, Bernstein was. You were lucky to know him. But sometimes genius isn't enough."

"What did you tell him that was so earth shattering that you were able to reverse the fucking polarity of his brain and make him kill himself?" I said. I could tear this man apart with my bare hands, magick or no, j_____ or no.

I thought the wrong thing. *Or no.* I gave my bare hands the choice, and my Will left them. *Or no.*

Riley leaned over and whispered a few very potent words in my ear. It was a sentence, a very dense sentence, that summed up years of his life, and all of his metaphysics. They were magic words, well rehearsed. They were lawyer words. Like Bernstein, I am a fucking genius, so I was able to apprehend all that he told me in an instant. To describe it might take a few more words than he used.

Riley's axiom was a basic one—one generally embraced at the very beginning of magickal practice. *The family, the clan, the state count for nothing; the Individual is the Autarch.* Straight out of *Magick without Tears.* But in the occult world, whatever is exoterically true must certainly be esoterically false, or at least so oversimplified so as to be inaccurate. So Bernstein studied and practiced for years, reached out to master after guru after *sifu* after intellectual, trying to find the deeper secret. The Key to It All.

Riley had been very straightforward—the occult truth is that there is no occult truth. That's what the Masons at the highest level were to have supposedly heard, once the bag came off their heads and the noose around their necks was loosened. *There is no secret.* Bernstein couldn't believe it.

So Riley proposed a bet. This was years ago, when they were all in school, with my father. Riley claimed that with the New Aeon dawning, Bernstein and my father would both learn that there was no revolutionary class, no everlasting nation-state, no eternal family, no timeless clan. All that is solid would truly melt into air, forever and ever, world without end. The year was 1968. A general strike had rocked France, the Tet Offensive revealed American imperialism as a paper tiger, and the streets ran red with blood sacrifices, from Nguyễn Văn Lém to Martin Luther King. Riley was a Goldwater man, and had offered the bet even as his candidate was going down to the greatest defeat in a political race that any of the three friends could remember. So of course Bernstein took the bet that in twenty years all the work of the left would be undone, across the world. My father watched them shake hands on it, and grew bitter to be excluded. Dad had always been an extraneous curve in their magic circle; he was the generous kid ready to pay for things in exchange for some company, the guy who could wire a hi-fi system with his eyes closed.

Bernstein also cheated. The painting was a working. A sigil designed to bring down capitalism itself. He poured his blood, sweat, tears, and soul—all literally—into the paint to perfect the spell. Where there was growth, there would be collapse. Bernstein would have preferred a communal order, but he wasn't against hedging his bet: a burning world of chaos and madness would have been as good as a win to him.

Riley was a kind person. He let the cheat slide, and said that he would just change the terms of the bet. When Riley won, he'd get the painting, as well as the five dollars they had put up. And by 1988, he had won. Reagan was completing his second term, China was on its way to becoming a capitalist superpower, and a little war in Nagorno-Karabakh showed that the Soviets hadn't supplanted ancient ethnic divisions with class consciousness and a perfected human nature. Bernstein surrendered the painting to Riley, but almost immediately my father asked to borrow it.

What is capitalism but a kind of cancer—society's economic cells growing out of control, threatening to consume so much that the entire system would die? My father wasn't convinced that the bet was lost—Nagorno-Karabakh? Really?—and thought he could use Bernstein's painting to arrest my mother's cancer. Instead, she sickened and died quickly. Bernstein's magic did work, just in the wrong way. He had misunderstood that capitalism is always about *creative destruction.* Even Leviathan is only a pawn in that destruction. The individual, just like Crowley said, will always win out over the herd, Riley explained. It's just a matter of Will.

Then Riley started saying other words. No, not words. Hardly even phonemes. A language older than tongues. He knew the lines that angels whispered in a person's ear when it was time to die. Hypnosis, the power of suggestion, weaponized neurolinguistic programming invented by the CIA and shared with major capitalists at the finest campaign fundraising dinners and cocktail parties—whatever it was, my own left hand began to shiver and quake. I tried to tell him to stop, but my throat was burning. Then I realized what to do. I focused on my right hand as much as I could, got it into my pocket, and pushed my finger into my spiked ring. Even as my left hand began to rise of its own accord—what was Riley ordering me to do to myself?—I chose the right-hand path.

I punched him in the neck. The air came out of him like a whistle, followed by a stream of blood.

And then I heard the sirens, then the grasping branches of the dead autumn trees were painted red, white, and blue. Fuck it, I ran down the dark street.

I looked back when I heard a thud and a cop car screech to a halt. I don't know if Riley's robe really rendered him invisible to agents of the state, but the black-and-white that winged him and sent him flying heels over head sure as hell didn't see him. Riley hit the asphalt hard, but not hard enough.

I ran across lawns and squeezed through hedges. I had managed to turn myself around completely, and had no idea where I was except that I was away from the sirens. A pair of headlights rolled past me, then a cheap old boat of a car pulled to a stop.

"Hey!" It was Roderick, his head sticking out the passenger-side window. "Get in! We've been looking for you. We came back to try to get you!"

I ran for the car—it was a two-door, so squeezing in behind Roderick involved some stunt work and yanking—and tumbled into the back. The driver punched the gas and I lost my balance before ever fully gaining it.

Roderick turned around in his seat and offered me a hand. "So, magick? Fucked-up shit, eh? Please meet my uncle. He was an army medic back in the day, so I thought he could help you."

I glanced over at the driver, who looked at me from the rearview mirror and smiled. Raymundo! My favorite person in this shithole town.

"Hello. I'm—" he started.

"The light of the world," I finished.

# 21.

Call it a bourgeois-sentimentalist flinch. Call it yet another failure of my Will to embrace my destiny as an Autarch of the self. Raymundo was ready for anything—we could drive to the airport *now* and get me on the redeye to Miami, and from there on a boat to Puerto Rico. He had cousins everywhere; he knew people. He and Roderick were cousins, and they had cousins of cousins, a matrix of cousins draped over the continent. Nobody would ever find me. Bank robbers from the independence movement would protect me on his say-so. But after just fifteen minutes of fruitless driving around, some frantic comparing of notes, and a quick examination of my neck, I had Raymundo drop me off at St. Charles, back in Port Jeff. I wanted to see my grandmother, the stupid old bitch. Visiting hours were long over, but I'm practiced enough in the art of invisibility to walk past a bored receptionist who can't even be bothered to look up from her Rosemary Rogers novel.

Grandma was unconscious, in a state deeper than sleep. Her bruises had ripened into strange purple fruit. I realized why my father had taken her. He knew I'd try to follow. *Oh, you got a better plan for money than her?* he'd shouted—that could have been about me, not Grandma's Social Security check. He had wanted to kill me at Bernstein's house, with Chelsea watching or assisting. The Abyssal Eyeballs show had had an ad hoc quality that stank of Plan B. Chelsea saw me at the first show, figured I'd come to the second, and whistled for Dad and his coterie. Aram and Karen probably tipped off Riley that I'd be there. And it wasn't as though I had any place else to go other than the show.

Except for where I was right then. And that's how the cops found me.

There was a trial, and it was a short one as I had no lawyer. I hardly made the papers, which was shocking given the sensationalism of it all. A punk-rock Satanist kills her father, his lover, and a former lover of her own in a kinky bondage performance art piece with twenty-five witnesses. Oh, and guest-starring a teenage dirtbag and a real-live Puerto Rican gangbanger type who killed a promising graduate student. But the newspapers didn't bite—certainly not *Newsday*, and not even the *National Enquirer*.

Geraldo Rivera, I would have even granted an interview to. *Call me, Geraldo!*

The dark hand of Riley was behind the media blackout, behind the utter absence of witnesses. I know because I was found guilty of three counts of second-degree manslaughter. The jury deliberated for just under two hours. My public defender was good for a few things. He got the judge to agree to allow me to wear a wig so that my Mohawk wouldn't prejudice the jury. And I got to stay on Long Island, in the county lockup, despite three three-year sentences to be served consecutively. *Wir bleiben hier.*

We are staying here? We have stayed here. Here I am, now.

Now, I am the only surviving relative of my grandmother, who is basically a vegetable with a beating heart, and whose nurse wheels her in to see me once a month. It would have been cruel, to her, to ship me upstate. Not that she remembers me at all. Every time she is placed across from me, she asks who I am, and what I'm doing in prison. Every time, I tell her. Sometimes I start by saying, "I killed my father." Sometimes I start by saying, "I killed your son." Either way, she cries throughout the telling of my story, and doesn't recognize herself in it, even when I tell of her scrabbling around in the dark while her son fucked a girl who looked just like me.

I get to wear my wig during visiting hours too. I think it helps Grandma deal with what I'm telling.

I never made *Newsday*, but Riley did. The Berlin Wall crumbled, as he predicted it would, just as I was put behind a thick set of walls here in the county lockup. I'm still far freer than the East Germans. I don't have to work and scrabble for my three hots and a cot—the Germans will, and they'll suffer for it. Riley made sure of that. He was all over the Eastern bloc, working with the leaders of the fledgling states to integrate property rights into the new laws and constitutions of their governments. If you tilt your head toward the east, and listen closely, and believe with all your heart in an unseen hand, you can hear the sound of poker chips being scooped up and moved from there to here.

Riley's personality profile appeared in the paper's Sunday magazine. He wasn't the cover story, but he got a color spread and four thousand words on what a genius he was. His right arm was a little chicken wing tucked up against his rib cage thanks to his accident, and the hole in his neck was obvious. Not as obvious as the permanent crease in my own, but I was pleased to have left my mark on his fucking throat. There was no mention of the occult, or even his college career save for his peculiar support of Barry Goldwater back in '68.

"When everyone else was into free love, I was into loving freedom." That's an actual quote from the piece. How could anyone not want to force open his adorable little mouth, and vomit down his throat?

Riley's hired wife was given a name in a caption: Dawn. They posed together, arm in arm, in their living room. On

194 **NICK MAMATAS**

the far wall behind them hung Bernstein's Tower painting. I am a fucking genius. The only one on Long Island, guaranteed. I always knew there was no such thing as j_____. But here's an inevitable happenstance I look forward to: Riley's been able to move about the world unseen, thanks to his magick robe that makes him invisible to state operatives. Well, he's working hard to eliminate the state and supplant it with a global marketplace. Soon, there will be no such thing as privacy, or subtlety. We'll all be tawdry celebrities on perennial benders, and releasing Rob Lowe–style sex tapes purposefully, to publicize our careers. One day, someone will find out about Riley, and expose him, and by extension me, to the world. *Occult* means *hidden*, but in the New Aeon of the all-encompassing market, there will be no hiding.

On the tier I make myself useful. I can read and write, and have become a scribe of sorts to some of the other girls. I keep my head down, and as this is county, most girls come and go pretty quickly, while I've become an institution. I'm a loner in a web of gang and extended family associations, but it's not so bad. If you keep your head down, and occasionally lick a little pussy, it's not so bad at all. Since women in prison are the lowliest, and sexiest, of class strata, every Maoist and anarchist group tries to recruit us. I get to read a lot of revolutionary newspapers—none of them have any idea why the Berlin Wall fell, and all of them seem happy to blame one another's lack of faith—and occasionally even receive a missive from Red Submarine. The endless repetition of the Mike Schmidt byline has been replaced by . . . nothing at all. Every article is anonymous. Now that's Taoist Marxism: the role of the party chairman is taken up by a blank space whose purpose it is to fill the role of the party chairman and keep everyone else out.

I still listen to Outrage every Wednesday night, on a little transistor radio I hide under my pillow. Nobody dares try to take it from me.

Roderick visited me once. He told me he was going to move to California, and that he doesn't dream of a great big snake anymore.

"What do you dream about?" I asked him.

He stared past me for a moment, as if looking over my shoulder and all away around the curve of the Earth to see into the back of his head. "Little snakes. Millions of them, necks tied to tails, like a net covering the whole world."

"What are you going to do in California?"

He shrugged. "Something with computers maybe?"

"Make a little money, that sort of thing?"

"Yeah," he said.

"Yeah," I said. "Cool." And that was that. My not cursing him out was all the thanks he was going to get, and he was grateful for it. He blew me a kiss on the way out.

Greg, never heard from him again. Eh, who could blame the kid, really?

My official prison job is highway cleanup. I can no longer Will myself to invisibility. The COs with their shotguns, the girls in our bright orange Oompa-Loompa jumpsuits, we're the only entertainment for the great and endless steel snake of Long Island Expressway traffic lines. Well, except for throwing shit out the windows. After my own failed experiment with it, I came to the conclusion that vegetarianism was a bourgeois affectation, something for people who benefit from current structures of oppression to agitate for. But now, after picking up my ten thousandth McDonald's wrapper— and after eating as many veiny prison-grade hamburger patties that make McDonald's taste like a Peter Luger steak—I was ready to eat the weeds.

And, as it turns out, I could. I was tearing up weeds on a traffic strip one day when I noticed a few different-looking greens.

"Hey, Michelle," I said, holding up a fistful. "Ever see anything like this before?" Michelle's an older woman, African American, a southerner. She got nailed selling her prescription medication to junkies at a five hundred percent markup. Because she was unincorporated and hadn't made a public offering of stock in herself, they threw her in prison with me. At home, she loved to garden and to cook for her hundred screaming nephews and nieces.

Michelle never had any little ones of her own, but only because she's an enormous dyke. I liked her.

"Bring it here, hold it out in front of you. Let me take a look," Michelle said. Michelle always shouted like a third-grader at the school play when among the COs, so they wouldn't beat her up. She was very worried about her teeth. Prison dentures rarely fit well. She peered at the leaves. I let them go and the wind from a passing tractor-trailer took them to her; they fell like feathers at her feet.

"That's amaranth, Dawnie," she said. "The leaves. It'll flower soon."

"Amaranth grows wild on Long Island?" I was surprised.

Michelle shrugged. "You're from here, girl. Don't you know?"

"I couldn't even identify the stuff with a bunch of it in my hands, Michelle."

She chuckled. "Yeah, I guess you're right. It's weeds mostly, but some people eat it."

"I know."

The next day, I looked it up in the prison library. It's mostly law books and romance novels, but they do have some news-papers. Amaranth grows just fine on Long Island; there just isn't any. Or wasn't any, according to *Newsday*, until Hurricane Hugo shanghaied some seeds from the south and dumped them on our shores. Amaranth means "never fading." It was Bernstein's name for me. Hurricane Hugo destroyed his home, and sent so much of his occult knowledge to the four winds. There are no coincidences, I know that. In times past, I would have retreated to my room to contemplate the plant and its connections to my life, to the spinning of the world, to the class struggle, but these days it's hard to give a fuck about anything. I almost miss wiping Grandma's ass sometimes, miss driving the Rabbit, and definitely miss peering through windows made of something other than crisscrossed wires. I destroyed myself, and for what? The man who killed Bernstein is striding across the planet like a colossus, remaking it in his own image, and harnessing Bernstein's power to do it.

Another storm is coming. There's no highway duty today, because of Hurricane Bob. It—no, he—has already chewed through the Carolinas, Maryland, and Jersey, and left a billion dollars of damage in his wake. Destruction, but not creative destruction, not capitalist destruction, and now Bob is bearing down on Long Island. I cannot help but picture him as Killer BOB from *Twin Peaks*, entire towns grinding between his big tombstone teeth. *Twin Peaks* was a favorite on the tier last year. We have a TV, HBO even, but it's not like we each get a tube in our cell. There's the tier proper, and its row of cells, a slim walkway surrounding it that we all have access to when the doors open in the morning, and another, larger, cage around all of us. On the other side of *that* cage, bolted to the far wall, is the TV. Good luck trying to get the remote control from whatever badass has claimed it for the day. When the batteries die from the incessant clicking around, we have to wait a day or three for one of the COs to replace them. One time the TV was stuck on TV-55 for a week. I was surprised there were no suicides.

Our hosts in county government have no idea what to do about Bob. He's roaring toward us like he's looking to break me out of here. Are we prisoners to be evacuated, or will only the good citizens of Riverhead and the coastal areas of Long Island be shepherded to safety? I hope the hurricane grinds the island down to a sandbar. I hope motherfuckers drown in their cars on the highway as they try to escape to Manhattan. O Leviathan, crash against the shore and send waves to bury us all.

"He maketh the deep to boil like a pot: he maketh the sea like a pot of ointment!" I shout, from my cell, to the group that is always gathered closest to the tier's TV. "Leviathan!" This is one way I'm able to keep my roommate from spending too much time in our cell.

And another storm is coming, one that even interrupts TV coverage of Bob, my new friend and, I hope, lover. It's a storm of steel riding through clouds of diesel. The girls on the tier are frantic over it. The two TVs on the tier are calling it the August Coup. Soviet hard-liners have called in the tanks, to save socialist society from glasnost, from perestroika. "Oh Lord, oh Lord!" one of the girls cries. "It's the end of the world! The storm, the tanks—Satan is walking the Earth!" She's right, and I want to tell her so, but her conception is so oversimplified as to be inaccurate. She has no idea what will happen next, but I'm pretty sure I do. I write it down with my little golf pencil and give it a day to see if my prediction comes true.

Boris Yeltsin, a capitalist alcoholic, climbs one of the tanks and gives a stirring speech. Like magick, the troops change sides. The girls go wild, hooting and pumping their fists. They're in fucking prison in capitalist America, and they still believe every stupid lie about freedom the television tells them. I give myself a gold star for my accurate forecast. Maybe later, when the CO turns the TV off for the night, they'll go back to their gang formations and to their grand hobby of broom handle sex to pass the time. That night, to the echo of someone's orgasmic screaming, I look up in the ceiling and think about how useless it is to be correct sometimes. It's so difficult to do the right thing, even when you can sense the spirit of the age, even when you believe you know where the waters of history will flow.

But then I think of my father's face and realize that the red smear across the boiled bones of his skull was the last thing I was ever sure of.

## ACKNOWLEDGEMENTS:

Once again, there are far too many people to thank, but these are the people I remember. First there's Michele Rubin, late of Writers House, who encouraged me to write a "boy book" for the YA market. I finally said, "How about *Harriet the Spy*, but she's a punk rocker and into Crowley and Trotskyism!" and then I didn't have to hear about the boy book too much anymore. Rachel Edidin loved the idea though and acquired it for Dark Horse, and Jemiah Jefferson got the book from hard drive to storefront. Molly Tanzer, Jason Ridler, and Kenneth Wishnia had a number of useful comments for me. The blogger known to me only as keith418 regularly shares his insights into the intersection of the political and the esoteric on his online journal, many of which I liberated and détourned for my own aesthetic ends.

And I must thank some people whose names I don't even remember. Once upon a time, in 1989, there was a comic shop called Flashpoint, and the cashier had something to do with a new fanzine-style political/culture rag called *The Long Island Alternative*, the first issue of which was available for free in the store. I got it, read it over and over till it fell apart in my hands, and then I wrote a little essay called "Schmucks for World Peace" and sent it in. They published it. I was seventeen and in high school. I was paid in copies and a subscription to the magazine, and ever since then I've been doomed to write. If you had anything to do with the magazine, or that comic shop, thank you.